Cold Mirrors

∴

PAT,
Thanks for the
support!
ENJOY THE STORIES! *
All the best,
C.J. Liney
x

☆ = power of suggestion

other titles by CJ Lines:

Filth Kiss

COLD MIRRORS
CJ LINES

ADRAMELECH

First published 2011 by
Adramelech Books
London, England
www.adramelech-books.co.uk

Copyright © CJ Lines 2011
www.cjlines.com

The right of CJ Lines to be identified as the author of this work has been asserted by him in accordance with the Copyright, Designs and Patents Act 1988.

All rights reserved. No part of this publication may be reproduced, stored in or introduced into a retrieval system or transmitted, in any form, or by any means (electronic, mechanical, photocopying or otherwise) without the prior written permission of the publisher.

ISBN 978-0956799401

Design Claire Peters
Cover photography Benjamin Whitley
Cover model Minnie Walker

Duplicity first published in *Graveyard Rendezvous* magazine #31, 2005

Lambkin first published in *Tiny Terrors* anthology (Hadesgate Publications), 2006

Emmeline first published in *Unspeakable Horror from the Shadows of the Closet* (Darkscribe Press), 2008

Come Die With Me first published in *Lionsgate Fright Club* magazine #1, 2009

Clown Stations first published in *Lionsgate Fright Club* magazine #3, 2010

In memory of Sebastian Horsley
1962 - 2010

11	The Trending
38	Debut
72	Clown Stations
74	Stop Press
80	Emmeline
84	Come Die With Me
92	Lambkin
120	The Monkey House
128	Nostalgia Ain't What It Used To Be
152	Gaijin
158	Patrick O'Hare: King of the Freaks
170	Duplicity
178	Emerson's Last Stand, or, Keeping Up With The Joneses
184	In Every Dream Home A Heartache

The Trending

·:··:·

The vending machine was broken on the morning I met Oscar and the day we destroyed the world.

I remember this distinctly because I'd taken to having a cup of coffee to warm my hands for the walk across campus. On that morning, however, I didn't have any and my fingertips felt tortured by the time I reached the computer lab. December in Vermont, for the record, is *cold,* and I had no idea where my gloves could be. It was still Christmas week although, to be honest, I'd lost track of exactly which day. Intensely working on my thesis had meant that some days lasted for two sunsets while others never even saw one. None of the people left on campus seemed to be adhering to a normal schedule either so we'd all kind of fallen into a gentle but jittery chaos, occasionally passing one another in the corridors or by the vending machine to nod an awkward hello.

The vast majority of students and teachers had gone home for the holidays, either eagerly or reluctantly to spend time with their families. The only ones left were the misfits and losers and, that year, I felt like the biggest loser of all. It'd been three months since I'd lost Mom, Dad and Abby in the accident and, truly, they were all I had. For the first couple of weeks after it happened, I didn't really think much about it. I carried on as normal. I'd seen the wreck that was made out of the Ford my dad had owned since as far back as I could remember and it just looked like meaningless bent metal. It was only in the third week that the memories of childhood visits to the zoo and hazy vacation road trips down to Illinois came flooding back. Then one night, there I was, blackout drunk and banging on the door of the police impound, screaming to see that damn car again. It suddenly felt imbued with a power that threatened to consume me if I didn't touch it. It felt like all I had left of the people I loved most and I wanted part of it as a talisman, to carry with me and protect me from the flood of grief that was already consuming me. The cops wouldn't let me have so much as a fleck of paint off it. They drove me back to college and put my sorry drunk ass back in bed.

The weeks after that were the blackest. Days and days of not eating; of crying until the skin around my eyes was raw and peeling; of howling at the wall of my dorm room until Jen next door came round to tell me, as politely as she could manage, to please try and keep it down. I missed Mom and Dad like Hell and it hurt even more to think of Christmas coming up and a what pointless, empty day that would be without them to provide the customary rituals of joy.

By the start of December, my grief had fully metamorphosed. It was as though it had begun as a gas cloud of confusion, turned into a flood of anger and then eventually solidified to a spear of pain sticking right in my heart. At least this last phase made it easier to carry with me as, slowly, I started to crawl back into my daily routine.

With newfound clarity of thought, it struck me that, of the three of them, I missed Abby the most. When I thought about Mom and Dad, I found it hard to get past Christmas but, with

Abby, my entire future felt like a horrible abyss and I would've done anything to just run backwards, away from it; anything to avoid falling in.

Abby and I had met in my Freshman year, many dreams ago, and it's almost a sick irony now when I recall my first impression of her. 'This girl could break my heart if I let her,' I'd thought to myself.

Still, I was reluctant to let her in. I'd had girlfriends before and I'd been hurt before but, by the time I'd started at UVM, I thought I'd steeled myself pretty well and was maybe even a little cocky about not needing or wanting a serious relationship. Then after just one afternoon spent with Abby – who was, like me, majoring in Theology – all the guile had melted and my defences were moot. I was hopelessly in love. I loved Abby like I'd loved no one else and the idea of ever even trying to love anyone again now felt as alien and as hopeless as trying to breathe underwater. The fact that Abby loved me back remains the most humbling flattery I'm ever likely to know.

Again, it sounds sick to say now, but Abby was the most genuinely *alive* person I've ever known. She was always laughing loudly; a contagious, uproarious laugh that could defuse even the most volatile of situations. She was always curious to find out more about everything. The crazier the subject matter and the harder she found it to believe, the more she wanted to understand it hence her presence, as a staunch atheist, in a Theology class. In most situations, you could rely on Abby to ask the questions that everyone was thinking but no one dared speak. More incredibly, she could make even the most hard-lined or controversial enquiries appear light and innocent. She was the most confrontational person I'd met and yet she never upset anyone.

To ease the sense of my loss, I became obsessed with items I'd taken from my parents' house when I'd gone there to handle the funerals and all the associated paperwork. I couldn't bear to stay longer than absolutely necessary but I filled a box with significant junk; my dad's baseball glove, some of my mom's hair bands, Abby's clothes and a bottle of her perfume. I would spend hours each day fondling, smelling and clutching them to myself, trying not to lose any memories and pretending their owners were still alive. It was while pondering the extent of my devotion to these objects that I hit on the idea for the thesis that would, I hoped, exorcise some of my pain as well as help me regain focus on my class.

I decided to explore the subject of holy relics and, more specifically, their origins. Who or what takes an everyday object and attributes to it the power to make the blind see, the lame walk or, in my case, the grieving feel a little less torment for a few precious moments? Was there really such a difference between a piece of wood from The True Cross and the silver cross pendant that Abby had worn on the night she died (which I now wore myself around my neck)? Both possessed great powers for those who believed in their magic. It was almost ironic that she'd only bought the thing to try and convince my parents that she was a good Christian.

Stumbling between the campus library, the computer lab and my dorm for a week, I barely noticed the student population dwindling until one morning when I woke up and saw that the snow had started. Outside my window was a thick snowfall that made the college buildings blend spectrally into their surroundings. Huge flakes still fell from the sky and, when I stepped outside, I could almost hear them hit the ground. The holidays had well and truly kicked in.

This isolation propelled me further into my studies of relics and into some shady areas which, months before, I would probably have shied away from. There was no denying it though. My Christian faith had wavered since the accident and now I felt ready to explore just about anything with an open mind. Besides, everything natural and supernatural was God's Will and God's Creation. The only difference between Jesus healing the sick and Crowley summoning demons was the subjective difference between good and evil.

It was with this logic in mind that I started seeing patterns throughout many theologies, all relating to relics. Magical objects tended to work when in the presence of large groups of believers. In order to channel their supernatural properties, a collection of like minds had to work hard in the natural world. I studied faith healers from Jesus Christ to contemporary TV evangelists and found their methods of working to be similar to those who walked darker paths. Using the internet from the computer lab, I vigorously researched the rituals of cults from the Thelemic Knights to Thee Temple ov Psychick Youth and found all could be traced back to a single element: the power of many minds working in harmony to achieve magic. The same applied even in the darkest of arts, like Spiritualism or Black Masses.

When I thought about the power of Abby's silver cross to fill me, if only briefly, with all the feelings of love I had for her, it made me giddy to think what it could do if my mind were working in conjunction with others feeling the same. Could we all feel the same love and comfort? Would it mean Abby's cross could heal grief for all of us, if there were thousands focusing on its power? Of course, such thoughts were verging on hokum but somehow I managed to channel them into what I felt was a coherent, if not outright brilliant, thesis.

150 pages wrote themselves in no time and, in the end, I was frantically chopping entire paragraphs out in order to make room for conclusions. Then the block hit. I simply couldn't find my point. I circled it for days but, unable to make a landing substantial enough to be worthy of the research preceding it, I just spent hours in the lab, staring at the blank screen, chugging down soda, making exasperated noises and trying to ignore the only other guy in the room.

I'd seen the guy every day that I'd been coming to the lab over Christmas but had made a point of not talking to him, as making new friends was very low down my list of things to do. He was bespectacled and although his brown hair, tied back into a ponytail, always looked clean, his t-shirts were stained with sweat and food and his wiry frame and diminutive stature made him appear unnervingly childlike, despite his beard. On any given day, he usually worked on three monitor screens at once; what I assumed was his personal laptop and two college-owned desktops. Whenever I'd walked past and glanced at his two desktop screens, I'd been confronted by page upon page of unintelligible programming code. It was intimidating.

However, on that one snowy morning, with numb fingertips, no coffee and a mounting frustration over my inability to write, I decided to just go talk to him. I hadn't actually formed a word with my mouth for probably well over a week at this stage and even I realized this wasn't healthy. So I walked over and introduced myself.

'I'm Jack,' I said, clearing my throat and extending my hand. 'Figured I should come say hi, given we're the only guys here.'

He turned slowly towards me and squinted as if to adjust his eyes to something that wasn't on a screen. 'Oscar,' he said, shaking my hand. His palm was damp. 'Computer Sciences. Puzzles, games and algorithms.'

'Theology,' I replied.

'Woah,' he flinched. 'You're not one of those Jesus freaks, are you? Sorry. I just mean, like, if you are, no disrespect, but I'm not interested, man. Kinda busy here.'

I realized that I hadn't cut my hair or shaved since the accident and that I was wearing a prominent silver cross. The comical absurdity of my cultish appearance suddenly hit me and made me laugh out loud. 'Nah, you're cool,' I said when I'd finished laughing. 'I'm not going to push anything on you. I just, uh, haven't shaved for a bit. Been busy with this thesis I've been writing.'

Oscar nodded, tentatively, as though he didn't believe me. I decided to make a peace offering of sorts.

'I'd buy you a coffee but the machine's broken.'

'It's all good. I got Mountain Dew.'

'Hope you don't mind my coming over,' I said. 'I'm just starting to feel a bit crazy. Had my head down in this thing all week and not slept much.'

'Sucks to be you,' he said. 'So what's it about?'

There was something convincingly curious in his voice as he asked this that told me he'd been craving some company too so I started talking. When I looked up at the clock again,

I noticed that nearly ten minutes had passed while I'd explained my thesis to Oscar.

'Uh, sorry. I... I guess it's been a while since I talked to anyone.'

'Heavy,' he murmured. 'It's cool though. I can dig all that stuff. Magic, y'know.'

'So what is it you're doing here?' I said, changing the subject and gesturing towards the screens of code. 'Is this for your thesis?'

'This?' he laughed. 'Nah, this is just fun.'

'Looks it,' I replied, under my breath.

'Do you know Magewar?'

'I think I saw a commercial for it. It's an online game, right? Like Dungeons & Dragons or something?'

He shrugged. 'I guess. They're both role-playing games. Magewar is a lot bigger though. It's all user-generated content and there are, like, millions of people all over the world who play it online, write the scenarios and program stuff for it.'

'And that's what you're doing here?'

'Yeah. I program, like, costumes and weapons mostly. Really cool stuff. See, the best thing about Magewar is that it has its own economy. There's this made-up currency that you buy with real US dollars and, long story short, guys like me can make real money making and selling virtual items. The cooler the stuff I code, the more cash I get.'

'Wow.'

'How do you think I'm paying my way through college?' Oscar grinned.

'So how long does it take to make this stuff?'

'Depends. Right now I just finished work on this golden,

jewel-encrusted mace. It's not that much better than a regular mace but it looks way cooler and works well with certain characters' magical attributes. Something like that usually takes a couple of days to put together.'

'And how much money do you get for that?'

'For that?' He shrugged again. 'I'm about to give it away. I sometimes do stuff just for kicks. I got a lot of followers on Twitter 'cos of all the Magewar stuff I do and sometimes I like to just mess around a bit. Look at this.'

I leaned in as he pulled the Twitter homepage up on his laptop; a social networking site that I was vaguely aware of but hadn't used.

'You know Twitter?'

'Not really. I know you just type stuff to the world, like what you had for breakfast.'

He rolled his eyes. 'Yeah. Well, you see these things here, with the hash tags at the start?'

I looked at where he pointed on the screen. It read:

#joejonasishot #3wordsafterdinner #heavyweather #OMG #teamjojomonkey #glee

'Uh, yeah. Looks great.'

'These are trending topics. When anyone looks at the front page, this is what they'll see. They're the most popular things that people are tweeting about. Some of it's, like, last night's TV or whatever, sometimes it's a private joke that spirals out of control, sometimes it'll be real news, like if someone dies or something. But basically, when you post something on a particular topic and put the hashtag at the start, that topic can 'trend' if enough people tweet or retweet it.'

'What's retweeting?'

'You just copy and paste what someone else has written. That's how I give away my stuff sometimes. Like this one time, I got people to retweet a hashtag with my name in it – #oscardash. I said if we could get it as a trending topic, I'd give away this, like, skeleton tunic I'd made for Magewar.'

'Did it work?'

'Hell yeah, I've got mad followers.' He laughed. 'Seriously, my name was in lights before, like, five minutes had passed. Everyone who logged onto Twitter – and we're talking millions here, my friend – saw Oscar Dash's name in the trending topics. Best thing is, these things go viral from there. Once #oscardash is a trending topic, you then get all these idiots tweeting things like 'who is #oscardash?' or 'what is #oscardash?' and it trends some more! My name was up there for nearly two days.'

'Wow,' I said. I'd been largely quiet as Oscar had talked. Partially out of respect, given how patiently he'd listened to me ramble about my thesis but also because my brain was taking it all in and making some unexpected connections.

I don't know if it was just because I'd been concentrating so intensely on my thesis that it was too difficult to tear my mind away from it. Or maybe it was something else. Either way, all I could think, as Oscar explained Twitter and its trending topics, was that this was almost exactly the same as all the magical rituals I'd been researching. It was a collection of minds focusing and concentrating on one item, in this case a word or phrase, and changing its state from the mundane and commonplace (a regular tweet) into something more special (a trending topic).

'I just need to think of a phrase to get them to retweet. I only used my name once and then a bunch of cheap plays on it but I'm running out of jokes.'

'Can I give you one?' I asked.

'Sure, what've you got in mind?'

'#rainonvermont'

'Rain on Vermont? That's, uh, random.'

'It's just something I was thinking. Probably just because I've got my head so deep in all this stuff I've been writing but I was just wondering if the power of all those people focusing on those words, all of those people typing them, could maybe work as some kind of incantation?'

'To make it rain?'

'Yeah.'

He laughed, a bit too loudly. 'You're about as crazy as you look, man. But what the Hell? I got nothing better.'

He typed quickly into the keyboard, clicked a few times and then leaned back in his seat. 'Okay, there we go. I posted a picture of the mace and told them to retweet #rainonvermont. I'll post a link to download the mace when it starts trending.'

'What now?'

'Now we just wait. Here, check this out. Irresistible, no?'

Oscar showed me first a picture of the golden mace he'd created then showed me a muscle-bound wizard-like avatar he'd made, wielding it in various ways. This all took about five minutes but my mind wasn't concentrating on it. Instead, I was mulling over in my head whether or not I'd lost my mind trying to make it rain over Twitter. Although it seemed insane to think I could achieve something supernatural this way, it also felt strangely logical. All the accounts I'd been reading - holy men blessing relics, occultists summoning devils or

Victorians talking with the dead - were the same. The realms beyond ours had been reached with a combination of chants and rituals mixed with the power of many minds working in unison. Why shouldn't it work for me?

'How's it going on Twitter?' I asked.

Oscar switched windows and refreshed the homepage. The trending topics had changed slightly but #raininvermont wasn't there. He typed the phrase into the search box and suddenly a whole barrage of messages appeared from what seemed like hundreds of users all retweeting it.

He chuckled. 'We're getting there. See, I told you it moves fast.'

I couldn't sit still and wait so I excused myself and made for the bathroom. I was halfway across the lab when I heard two sounds in such quick succession and I couldn't tell you which came first. One was Oscar shouting 'Dude, it's trending!' and the other was perhaps the loudest thunderclap I'd ever heard.

I turned to face him and saw, through the window above his head, raindrops drumming against the glass. I looked him in the eyes and initially saw a flash of fear but it was followed by his noisy, throaty laugh.

'Well, that's fuckin' funny,' he said, chuckling away.

'I… I…' I couldn't finish my sentence and just stuttered, as the two of us walked towards the window and watched the rain. It was coming down heavily, already blending with the snow and starting to turn the perfect whiteness into a greyish sludge. My eyes bulged as I tried to comprehend what had happened.

'Chillax,' he said, putting his hand on my shoulder. 'It's just coincidence.'

'It can't be. We… we made this happen, Oscar! We did this!'

I realized that with my tired eyes, messy beard and long hair, I probably looked completely crazy as I barked this at him, so tried to compose myself.

'Look, I check the met websites,' he explained. 'They've all been saying it'll probably rain sometime this week, get shot of this snow. It's gotta go sometime.'

'But now? At the exact point it started trending?'

'These things happen. You're telling me you've never seen a coincidence before?'

Of course I had but this felt different. I decided not to answer him.

'This... This is it, Oscar. Don't you see? We made it rain. We have touched a realm beyond what most people will ever know.'

He chuckled. 'Whatever, dude. I've got a mace to upload.'

Oscar walked back to his desk, shaking his head. I watched the rain for about another minute and then decided I had to feel it for myself. Ignoring Oscar, I strode out of the lab and into the campus grounds without even stopping to put on my jacket. Once outside, I ran across the courtyard and let the rain soak my hair and my face.

'I made this rain!' I screamed. I threw my arms out wide and then pointed skywards. 'You! I made you!'

I was elated. I ran all the way back to my room, arms aloft, basking in the feeling that each drop of water that landed on me was not part of some meaningless storm but instead something brilliant, something supernatural that Oscar and I had summoned, had brought into this reality from another. I laughed maniacally as I turned the key in my door and entered my dorm room.

Once inside, I ripped my shirt and pants off and threw them

onto the floor. I soon lay naked on the bed and stared up at the ceiling, a million thoughts shooting around my head in different directions like fireworks. My thesis now had a whole slew of alternative conclusions. I contemplated everything. Whether or not what I'd done had been Christian. Words like 'technomancy' flashed through my mind alongside phrases like 'playing God'. Still, I wondered only briefly whether what I was doing had been right; these worries were eclipsed by the dizzying possibilities of what I could do next.

After a few hours of solitary brainstorming, I walked over to the sink. This was the first time I'd felt truly happy since the accident and I knew that now was when I had to break free from some of my grief. I grabbed a pair of scissors and began frantically cutting away at my hair and beard until both were eventually a manageable length. I used a razor to shave the remaining beard. I looked almost like myself again, albeit a slightly thinner, less tidy version.

As I studied my nakedness in the mirror, Abby's silver cross around my neck caught my eye and suddenly I started shaking. The extent of what had happened today all hit me at once and I nearly fell down. Was there a limit to what I could do using Twitter to create massive, virtual rituals of magic? Surely not. If I could make it rain, what was to say I couldn't raise the dead?

I laughed hysterically, clutching my wrist hard to stop my hands shaking.

'Abby,' I whispered into the mirror. 'Oh, Abby. Abby. Abby.'

Even the repetition of her name was beginning to feel like a magical incantation, as though I were already laying groundwork for what I knew I had to do.

'Abby, Abby, Abby, Abby…'

I pulled some dry clothes out of a drawer and put them on. I had to persuade Oscar to help me somehow and thus tried to compose myself and appear as sane as possible. Glancing at the clock, it seemed I'd spent all day lying in bed. It was already six in the evening and I hoped with all my heart that Oscar would still be there in the lab. I seized my umbrella and ventured back out into the rain. The slush was now a dark, brownish grey and was slippery underfoot.

When I got to the lab, I felt a surge of relief that was almost palpable as I saw Oscar's familiar frame still hunched over his laptop.

'Oscar!' I shouted, dropping my umbrella on the floor and bounding across the room towards him.

He spun around on his chair and looked at me without recognition. 'Uh, do I know you?'

'It's Jack! From this morning.'

The penny dropped. 'Ahhh. You look different without all the, uh… hair. You feeling okay?'

'Never been better.'

He nodded. 'Hey, you know #rainonvermont is still the top trending topic? 'Cos now everyone's, like, talking about how it's raining in Vermont and they're all using the same hashtag. It's pretty funny. I told you that's how these things work.'

I shook my head as if to say that didn't matter. 'Listen. I need to talk to you. I've had an idea.'

'Uh huh.'

'I want to try the trending topic thing again, but with something different this time.'

'Nah, sorry, man. It was fun while it lasted and all but I've got nothing else I want to give away at the moment and, besides,

I'm not sure I'm one hundred percent comfortable with encouraging you… You seemed a little, uh, wired after the rain thing this morning. No disrespect.'

'So you don't have anything? No, like, swords or flashy tunics or…?'

'Well…'

'C'mon, you've gotta! A guy like you? You've been plugged into those screens all week.'

'I've got a battering ram that shoots cannonballs that I've been working on but that's a special item. I could fetch at least a hundred bucks – that's real US dollars – for that if I sell it at the marketplace. Plus, it's a unique item. I can't just put up a download link on Twitter for everyone to take that one.'

'What if I pay you for it? I'll give you a hundred bucks, right here, right now.'

'To do what? You don't even play Magewar.'

'I'll pay you to stick it up on Twitter. A hundred bucks. For real.'

'I told you, I can't. It wouldn't work because it's a unique item.'

'What about if you… I don't know… if you… told them that the millionth person to retweet what I want you to retweet would get it? You'd send it to just them.'

'Hmm,' he thought about it. 'I guess I could run a script pretty simply that would tell me who that was. Plus, I suppose, if anything, that would make it trend even quicker. There'd be people retweeting multiple times because they'd want to make sure they were the millionth. But, nah, man. What is it you want to put up there anyway?'

'I want these words: "Abby McCullagh, come back to me".'

Oscar put his head in his hands. 'Oh, dude. You're kidding

me? You're doing all this to get a girl back? Seriously, you need to settle down and think about what you're d…'

'She's dead, Oscar. Abby's dead.'

He made a goldfish sound with his mouth.

'She died in a car accident with my parents three months ago.'

'No. No, no, no. This is just weird. Listen, I'm sorry but…'

'Please, Oscar. You said yourself that the rain thing was just coincidence. You don't even believe in any of this stuff. What harm can it do? It'll be the easiest two hundred bucks you ever make.'

'*Two* hundred?'

I nodded emphatically.

He sighed and looked at me for a few seconds, before staring me straight in the eye. 'Jack. I'm really sorry for your loss. Really. I can't even imagine what you're going through right now. I guess that's why you're acting a little… a little like how you're acting. But I don't know you and I don't want to get involved in your… whatever it is. It's not healthy and I'm sure as Hell not a guy you can rely on to help you get through this stuff. You depend on me and it's gonna make things worse. I'm a geek, Jack. I didn't become a Level 80 Paladin through having good people skills.' He laughed, drily.

'Oscar, please…'

'Let me finish. If I do this for you, for two hundred bucks, if I humor you and get a million retweets of what you're asking me for, I need you to promise – whatever happens – you're not ever going to ask me to do anything for you again. See the school shrink or something. Talk it through. I get the idea you've been bottling it all up and this isn't the way to release it.'

'So you're gonna do it?'

He sighed again, deeper this time. 'Sure. Give me five minutes to get some screenshots of the battering ram. You do know this is going to trend in no time? That ram is seriously sweet.'

A few minutes later and he'd made the tweet and, minutes after that, #abbymcullaghcomebacktome began shooting up the trending topics list.

'Aw, man,' he said, 'look at some of these tweets. '@oscardash: #abbymcullaghcomebacktome : Hey Oscar, what's up? She dump you? LMAO' Everyone thinks I'm doing this to get a girl back.' He shook his head. 'Lame, damnit. Lame.'

I put my hand on his shoulder. 'It's going to happen, Oscar. We've opened ourselves up to a realm beyond this one. We can do this. We can make this happen. We can bring her back, don't you see?'

He brushed my hand away and frowned. 'Sure, Jack. Sure. Hey, by the way, you might wanna go hit up the ATM for that two hundred bucks you owe me for destroying my online reputation.'

'Oh, yeah, sorry. I'll get it now.'

I walked to the desk where I'd left my jacket earlier, put it back on and walked out of the lab and down a corridor towards the nearest ATM on campus. My heart was pounding in my chest. My hands were still shaking. Was I really going to see Abby again? How was it going to happen? Would she just appear, right there in the lab? Would she appear by her graveside? Would she have clothes? Would she be corporeal? Suddenly, a thousand logistical questions popped up at once and I had a sinking feeling that I'd made a mistake, that I was crazy and attempting the impossible or, at best, that if I did bring Abby back, I'd never find her.

Just as I was about to put my card into the ATM, I heard a loud, low-pitched mechanical whine and all the lights in the corridor went off. The ATM screen flickered green and then turned to black.

'Abby?' I whispered, then felt like a fool for doing so. It was just a blackout. They were pretty common in Vermont when the weather was bad. It was just unfortunate timing for Oscar that it'd happened before I'd got his money. I was going to head back to the lab but then, from the top of the metal, riserless staircase leading to the upper floors, I heard a noise. It was hard to pinpoint at first. It sounded like a gasp, a sharp intake of breath, coming from somewhere above me.

I looked up through the steps and could see no one there. The staircase was very dark without electrical lighting, despite the huge glass wall behind it. Outside, with no streetlights working, all I could see was a sheet of even heavier rain than earlier. Almost all of the snow had turned to blackish puddles of slush now. The pattering of water on the glass sounded like dull white noise.

I heard the gasp again. This time it was less of a gasp, more of a sob. It sounded like a woman sobbing. As I tentatively climbed the stairwell, the sound became louder. It was definitely somebody crying. Maybe it was one of the other students who was here over Christmas and was scared of the dark?

'Hey? Hello?' I said. 'Are you alright? It's just a blackout.'

The crying continued.

As I reached the top of the stairs, I looked down the corridor of the upper floor and felt my stomach lurch. Had I eaten all day, it would've all come back up at that moment. Sitting against the wall, naked and with her head between her knees, was Abby. She was pale to the point of being lambent in the darkness. She was sobbing heavily. I couldn't believe what I was seeing so I walked carefully towards her, terrified that the apparition would disappear if I moved too quickly.

'Abby,' I whispered. 'Oh God, Abby. It's me, Jack.'

At that point, she raised her head and looked directly at me. Her eyes were watery and the green of her irises was paler than I remembered. 'Jack?' she whispered back to me.

I couldn't find the words to say to her at that moment.

'Where am I?' she asked. Her voice sounded tiny and cracked, almost inaudible.

'You're at school. I... I... brought you here. There was an... there was...' I didn't know what to say. I didn't know how much she knew, what she could remember. I was terrified of upsetting her or saying the wrong thing and having her vanish.

'I'm cold, Jack. I'm so cold.'

She had always been small in stature but her personality had masked that as much as possible. Now she was so vulnerable and fragile looking, she seemed like a tiny, sickly child. I took off my jacket and went to put it around her shoulders. It hung there for a few seconds and then seemed to fall through her and onto the floor. As it passed downwards, she shivered and groaned as if it hurt. Again, my stomach lurched. What was she? What had I done?

'I'm sorry... I... I don't know what to do... Maybe, maybe you'll get stronger as time passes. Maybe you'll become more... more... corporeal...'

She looked up at me with those damp, sad eyes and asked, 'What am I, Jack?'

I felt like crying too because I had no answer. Also I felt

like crying because I was so happy she was back, that we were together again.

'Abby,' I said, as softly and calmly as I could. 'Stand up. We'll get you back to my room and we'll try to figure out what's going on, okay? Let's just get back to my room. Ready? It's going to be alright.'

She stood up and covered herself with her hands. I saw now that her skin appeared slick, as though covered in a light condensation. I reached out to touch her back. She flinched and moved away as my fingertip approached but that was enough for me to feel how cold she was. It was a cold like nothing I'd felt before and my skin burned with it for minutes, even after such brief contact. It made the numb feeling in my fingers from the courtyard earlier that morning seem warm and comforting by comparison.

I walked back down the stairs and towards the exit, turning back every few seconds to make sure Abby was following me. She was still sobbing and covering herself and walking awkwardly, as though she'd only just learned how. I hoped that this disorientation would wear off soon, that it was just like some kind of jetlag from traversing between the realms of the supernatural and the natural. It scared me how little I knew about what she had gone through and what she was going through. All I wanted to do was help.

As we entered the courtyard, I felt the rain soak my shirt and remembered I'd left my jacket lying on the floor upstairs. I swung round, contemplating whether I should go back to get it and saw, with shock, the effect the rain was having on Abby. She was crying loudly now and flickering like a bad television reception.

'Jack! Jack! It hurts... It's... It's like needles going through me!' she gasped.

'Oh God, Abby. Abby. I don't know what to do.'

She began slapping at her skin and trying to brush away the rain. I wanted to help but was afraid to reach out and touch her again.

'Let's... Let's just move quickly.' I went to grab her but realized in time that it wouldn't work. 'Come on.'

I broke into a run and she tried to follow, still screaming and rubbing herself down. Eventually we reached my dorm room door. I fumbled to unlock it and we both fell inside. Abby was still flickering and, again, I was scared I would lose her; that she would disappear. I looked hard at her and tried to take in as much as possible, drinking in her presence. I noticed, peculiarly, that a mole on the left side of her forehead was no longer visible there but was now on the right side.

It was just then I heard the booming sound of laughter from behind the door. The electricity flickered back on inside the room and a light that I'd left on earlier came back to life. In the light, Abby was almost invisible so I immediately turned it off and plunged us back into darkness.

'Who's there?' I shouted to the door, as the laughter began again. 'Oscar, I'll kill you if this is you.'

The laughter continued.

'Abby, wait here,' I said. She was flickering less now. She nodded. I noticed thin trails of grey slime were oozing from her eyes down her face. She was crying.

'Jack,' she wept. 'I'm so cold. I'm so scared. I don't want to be here.'

'It's going to be alright, Abby. It's going to be alright.'

There was a loud banging sound on the door. Then, once more, laughter. This time the male laughter was accompanied by a high, almost screeching female voice that reminded me of my mom's.

'Go away!' I shouted but it didn't stop.

I flung open the door in a rage, ready to throw a punch but I nearly fell over when I saw who stood there, naked, glowing in the darkness of the corridor.

'Hello Jack,' my dad said. His skin was pallid and spotted with condensation and what little hair he had was pressed wet to his head like an oil slick. His face looked strange but I couldn't place exactly how.

'Dad…? Dad…?'

Part of me wanted to embrace him but another part was afraid. Something didn't look right. My dad had always just been a loveable lug; a kind-hearted man who liked nothing more than vintage muscle cars, a good baseball game and a barbecue in the summer. You'd know this just to look at him, with his kind eyes, his soft face… Now, his features were hardened. Twisted somehow. His eyes looked cruel.

I flinched and looked downwards. Crawling between his legs and laughing hysterically was my mother. Like Dad, she looked crazed and wrong. There was nothing loving or maternal about her whatsoever.

Inside the room Abby was screaming loudly now, covering her ears, the grey, viscous tears pouring from her eyes. Mom and Dad were laughing.

'You missed something in your research, Jack,' said Dad. 'But then you never were the brightest.'

My heart hurt. It was the first time my father had ever said anything remotely discouraging to me.

'With every blessing comes a curse,' he continued. 'Think about the artefacts you've been looking at and the way they work. The bones of a dead, tortured man are used to heal the sick. Burial shrouds as holy relics. Things that represent pain, death and horror in the natural world have benevolent properties in the supernatural world.'

This wasn't language my dad would ever use. I stood there, gaping silently, as he spoke, wondering who or what he was.

'There is a mirror world on the other side of your reality, Jack. That's where we go when we die. Behind the mirror, where everything is opposite.'

I nervously fingered Abby's silver cross that hung around my neck, my mind desperately trying to think of ways to reverse what had happened. What I'd done. I wanted all three of them to leave at once.

'Everything's the other way around in the mirror world. Look at Abby. She's weak. She's terrified. She's absolutely nothing.'

Abby was pulling at her hair now and muttering to herself. 'I'm cold, Jack. I'm so fucking cold.'

'Sometimes, people try to look behind the mirror, they try to bring things back. Look at the faith healers, how often they're disgraced, how they fall from grace, cast out of their flocks with some scandal. It's because they've taken something that isn't theirs, that they're not supposed to have. It's the price they pay when the mirror world claims its toll. But Jack, you've done something so much bigger than that. Do you know how many people joined you in your little ritual?'

'N... No...'

'Over a million souls, Jack, all hammering at their keyboard, all hammering away at the mirror. They're still punching it in as we speak, all over the world. Well, I'm sorry Jack, but the mirror broke.'

'That's a lot of years of bad luck, son!' screeched my mom at my feet, laughing hysterically and rolling her inverted eyes back into her head.

'But… how… I just… I just asked for Abby back?' I stammered.

'You can't reach in and take what you want. You made a hole in the veil that separates our two worlds. How did you expect to control that? We've come through the wires, through the airwaves and we're here now. All of us. Look outside.'

I looked at the curtain that covered my window, afraid to draw it. I walked towards it and, closing one eye, pulled it open viciously, like I was yanking off a Band-Aid.

Outside, the night was lit up by naked white apparitions. There were thousands of them across the campus, crammed together like veal. Some sat on the floor, picking at themselves. Some were shambling aimlessly forward. Some were screaming silently. Some wept, others laughed. Some were climbing the walls of the college buildings. Others lay on the ground, trying without success to claw their way back under the earth. Some were trying to fight their way out of the crowd. It seemed pointless. The crowd stretched as far as I could see.

I turned back to face my dad. Behind him in the corridor were more of them, walking in line.

'Oh God, what have I done?'

My dad put his fingers in his mouth and began to stretch it open. His face seemed malleable like rubber. He turned to me so I could see almost all the way to his throat. Inside his throat was an almost blinding white light. It pulsed, hypnotically and, for a second, I was unable to tear my eyes from it.

'NO!' Abby howled, deafeningly, and ran to the door, fighting her way past my parents and into the throng.

'Abby, wait!' I shouted. I wanted to run after her but was too scared.

My dad closed his mouth, as about five or six of the apparitions – all dead-eyed, doughy, anonymous strangers – tried to make their way into my dorm room. I slammed the door shut and stared at it for several seconds, expecting them to just float through it. Nothing happened. I could still hear them outside but they weren't coming in. They just stood outside yelling all at once until whatever they were shouting became incoherent.

I sat down on the bed and cried, trying to cover my ears and stop the sounds of the dead screaming all around me.

I have slept fitfully since then because the noise won't stop. All I hear is the sound of the dead everywhere. I have written and rewritten my account of the last few days, trying to recall each and every detail as accurately as possible so that I might find a way to send them back. It hasn't worked. I thought about setting up a Twitter account and begging for people to retweet incantations, desperate phrases to send the dead back to where they belonged, but I couldn't bear to head back to the computer lab. Besides, I didn't know if there would even be anyone to receive my requests.

Inside my room, it was impossible to know what was happening outside. Were the dead claiming the souls of the living? Or were they just wandering endlessly amongst us, trying to find their place or their way back? Or was it a little of both? It was impossible to know. I was too scared to open the door and be amongst them, too scared of their icy touch, their eerie glow and their longing eyes. Every time I peeked behind the curtain, hoping to see Abby out there among them – frightened for her wellbeing – I saw more of them outside. An endless procession marching across campus to God knows where. When I opened the window, the air streaming in was freezing. Vermont was a necropolis. I saw no evidence that any living soul still existed.

I would've killed myself but knowing now what lay beyond, that prospect seemed even worse than living with this. So instead, I will keep writing my story. I need to somehow get it onto a computer, to send it to the internet. I keep hoping that someone, somewhere is alive. That maybe one day someone will read this and can help reverse what I've done and send the dead back. We have to send them back.

#sendthemback - please retweet.

Debut

∴

PART ONE : CORNWALL

From the moment he had arrived at Wadebridge station, Henry Herbert's circumstances worsened. Not only had the rain been torrential all morning, disrupting the running of the railroad, but a goods train carrying a penned wooden carriage full of pigs had almost overturned as it pulled into the station just in front of Henry's own train. No major damage had been caused but one of the pen gates had swung open and the pigs had escaped, causing panic on the platforms. By the time his train was ready to pull into the station, Henry could still see from the window a cluster of frantic silhouetted figures rushing to catch the swine; a dark blur in the downpour. The station was a frenzy of squealing and screaming. Men in long coats were slipping and sliding as they tried in vain to control the situation. Henry took his cases and stepped warily onto the platform, but was nearly knocked down by a large, soaking black pig that let out a shriek as it streaked past. For a second, it looked up at him with beady dark eyes that appeared irrationally malevolent. Luckily, the beast was gone within seconds, galloping off into the rain.

His heart racing, Henry wove his way outside and hoped he would still be able to find a good coachman to take him to Polzeath, even though he was running a few hours later than he had planned. There were few carriages left outside the station and Henry contemplated the idea of just finding a nearby inn, whiling away the remainder of the day there and continuing his journey in the morning. Unfortunately, neither his schedule nor his financial circumstance would permit him the luxury. Henry had been sent to Polzeath by Cassius Crabb, a fearsome individual renowned for his tightness with money and universal impatience with all and sundry; especially his employees. Crabb's unpleasantness was tempered, however, by his charm towards those he deemed useful, and a formidable skill for discovering stage talent and promoting it. It was thanks to Crabb that the Paragon Theatre of Varieties was fast becoming one of the most popular music halls in the East End. His entertainment bills - an intoxicating mixture of singers, ballerinas, puppeteers, acrobats and actors - were acclaimed throughout the papers of the capital, and many of his hand-picked performers had moved on to be major theatre stars. Of course, even with an keen eye like that, Crabb's kind of success could only be borne from a certain level of ruthlessness and guile; two crafts at which he was a master.

Still, Henry felt lucky to have his position as Cassius Crabb's assistant. Born in Limehouse to the music hall actress Nora Herbert, the fatherless Henry would have been destined for an urchin's life, had it not been for Cassius Crabb's obsession. The young Crabb was enchanted by Nora's performances and would attend each of them, sending notes and flowers to her on a near nightly basis, desperate in his pursuit. Eventually, she was charmed and the two of them began to court. They were due to be married in the spring of 1867, but Nora failed to survive the winter of the previous year, when her life was claimed by consumption. Crabb was devastated and vowed to educate, employ and raise the young Henry himself as an act of devotion to his lost lover. It was also at this point in his life that Crabb's rise to fame truly began; his fierce energies were now fixed solely on his work.

Henry had been Crabb's assistant for as long as he could remember. The work was often frightful and he would be active most hours of the day, running errands, rounding up drunken performers and generally carrying out the dirtier end of business for his employer. Debt collection and pre-emptive scouting for talent in the rougher East End haunts were a specialty. This would often result in black eyes from alehouse proprietors, slaps from local bawds and, once, a broken leg from an angry sailor who left Henry the limp that stayed with him for the rest of his life. His reputation amongst the denizens of the East End was that of a pathetic, half-crippled worm dangling slimily from the coat tails of his superior. He had few friends. Henry was well aware of the way he was perceived and wanted urgently to remedy this. He had been saving the money Crabb had paid him. When he had gathered enough, he would make an honest woman of his true love, the unacclaimed actress Sarah Seabourne, and they would open their own theatre, in the comparatively opulent West End. These were his big dreams and he was determined that they would one day become reality.

For the time being though, he remained Crabb's whipping boy and had been sent to Cornwall to make an offer to Peter and Oliver Tarny, a celebrated father-and-son puppeteer act whose reputation for uncanny craftsmanship and inventive performance was gaining momentum even as far as the capital. Crabb wanted them in his stable at the Paragon before any rival promoters had a chance to snap them up and had thus sent Henry on an urgent journey to the coast to ensnare their interest.

As he stood outside Wadebridge station, contemplating his fate, Henry noticed there was one rickety carriage left waiting, manned by a stout, ruddy-faced man whose nose hair seemed to meld into his beard, creating an almost lupine effect.

'Vincent Vickers, at yer service,' he said, doffing his cloth cap as Henry approached.

'I was wondering if you might be able to take me to Polzeath,' the other began. 'I know the weather is frightful, but I really do need to get there posthaste.'

'That's awlright with oi, zir. Why don't you juz climb in?' Vickers smiled, his teeth an array of yellow and brown stumps, even dirtier than his carriage.

Although the rain was still torrential outside, Henry felt reasonably safe in the cab as it trotted out of the cobbled streets of Wadebridge and into the gloom of the countryside. The pattering on the roof lulled Henry into a light slumber.

He awoke unexpectedly with the shock of a loud noise and a jolt as the carriage rocked harshly from side to side. Glancing out of the window, he found it was dusky outside. He squinted to take stock of his surroundings then nearly screamed when he saw the carriage was only a short distance away from a steep cliff edge. Henry heard the neighing of the horses and held on to the door handle as, once more, the carriage swayed. He didn't dare look as the wheels seemed to spin ever nearer the ledge and he felt himself bobbing up and down on his seat involuntarily. The wind was shrieking through a gap in the carriage door.

'Help!' he shouted, in blind panic. 'Help!'

'Don't be afraid, zir!' came Vickers' voice from somewhere. 'Oi've got it!'

Henry ducked and covered his head as the carriage veered left, away from the path and went trundling into a small wood. A scattering of spindly-limbed trees brushed the roof of the carriage, evoking an image of skeletal fingers scratching against the wood of a coffin lid. Henry closed his eyes and imagined the carriage as his own coffin. He could hear the horses becoming scared and Vickers shouting incoherent abuse at them. He was convinced he was going to die. The whole coach was shaking violently now. There was a yell, followed by an almighty jolt, and the carriage halted, flinging Henry to the floor. He caught his breath, brushed himself down and threw open the door to the carriage, incandescent with rage.

'What the Devil are you playing at?' he barked at Vickers, who was pale and sweating at the reins, clutching onto them for dear life.

'Zorry, zir,' he began breathlessly, blinking in the evening's half-light. 'Oi appear to 'ave mizzed the Polzeath Road. It waz rainin' awful 'ard back zere and oi did took the wrong one.'

'So where in God's name are we?'

Vickers seem to relax a little. 'We're near Polzeath, zir. Just came a long way, oi did. Wouldn't want be drivin' roond these cliffs by choice, zir. We over by the rookery, just a bit so'west o' the beach, oi believe. It be too dangerous to go on in thiz though, zir. We 'ave to wait 'til morning.'

Henry was horrified. There was a chilly mist rising from the grounds of the woods and he felt himself stiffen with fear and revulsion at having to spend the night here. He didn't even feel he could trust this Vickers character not to roll him in his sleep.

'If I am that near to Polzeath, I shall simply walk there and find myself an inn.'

Vickers winced. 'Zir, oi really wouldn't do that, if oi were you. It's goin' be a cold night. You'd be zafer in here, you would.'

There was a lengthy silence. The two men were still catching their breath and the forest had darkened rapidly. Henry wasn't used to such pitch black. Even the murkiest streets of the East End were faintly illuminated by a gaslight glow from somewhere, whether a main road or a brothel window. Here there was only the oppressive murk of the night; the moon itself lay hidden behind dense rain clouds. He could barely even see the coachman in front of him.

'So be it,' he snapped and returned to the carriage, using his hands to guide him. Vickers appeared shortly afterwards, pulling a blanket from a hidden compartment and offering it to Henry. It smelt even worse than the coachman himself, so Henry declined and wrapped himself up in his Chesterfield coat instead.

'Goodnight, Mr. Vickers,' he said curtly, curling into his corner of the carriage and closing his eyes.

He could hear the squawking and fluttering from the nearby rookery. It sounded almost lunatic and reminded him of the horrible pigs running loose in Wadebridge station. He remembered the evil gaze of the black pig and shivered. The wind was blowing harshly and tree branches were bending outside, rustling their leaves noisily, as if to mock Henry and deprive him of sleep. The chill bit at his lips and eyelids as he pulled his coat tighter around him. This journey had been a disaster and he wished he were back in London. He focused his mind on the city and on thoughts of Sarah Seabourne, to calm himself. Eventually, he stumbled into broken, unsatisfying slumber.

※ ※ ※

Henry awoke with a start in the back of the carriage, short of breath and haunted by the misty tendrils of nightmare. He wiped a trail of saliva from his whiskers, shook his head and ran his fingers through his hair, slowly regaining a sense of reality. He drew back the graying chiffon curtain and peered out of the window. The carriage was moving at an acceptable speed again and the landscape was once more flat and reassuringly nearer to sea level. They appeared to be descending a gentle incline towards a beach and he knew this must be Polzeath. The September sun was shining bright and low in the sky. He wrenched the small window open and took in a breath of fresh sea air. It was quite the pleasant novelty; its crispness a stark contrast to the thick, heavy fog he was used to in London. As he rolled his shoulders and put his hat back on, the terrors of the previous night began to dissipate and sense of tentative well being blossomed in their place.

Vickers pulled the carriage to a careful halt on the edge of the beach and let Henry out. He said he would refuse any payment offered, owing to the inconvenience of the previous night, which was fine by Henry, as he'd no intention of paying the awful little man anyway.

Henry took his case and his cane and looked around. There

were several rows of houses and inns along the sea front and, with the tide low, the beach stretched out for a couple of miles. After scanning the sands for a few minutes, his attention was drawn to a small plateau of rock on the southwest side, elevated a few feet above the ground. Atop it was a red and green caravan with a curved roof. Besides the caravan, Henry could just about ascertain an unusual box-like structure. He decided to investigate and, as he limped towards it, he noticed a small crowd doing the same thing, emerging from various corners of the beach and promenade. They were mostly children, but a smattering of adults was milling around anxiously behind them.

Once the box was in view he saw a carved wooden sign atop it that read 'Tarny and Son's Littlest Theatre' and he smiled. His luck was clearly changing. As the children sat down in a semi-circle before the box, Henry clambered onto the platform and stood at the back, waiting for the show to start. The box was about six feet in height and painted green. Two short red velvet curtains hung from the top and covered the upper half. They opened to reveal a hole in the centre of the box, decorated with blue and white paper sunflowers. Two small marionettes stood still inside it, maybe seven or eight inches in height. Henry observed they were beautifully crafted and very lifelike, even if some of the features had been exaggerated for humorous effect and their ragged clothes were purposely ill fitting. A mechanical music box began to play Gounod's 'Funeral March of a Marionette' and the puppets comically attacked one another, painted hands flailing, wooden legs akimbo. They would fall on their backsides, then magically flip back up to life with a flamboyant thrashing of limbs.

Even Henry, jaded from so many years of working for Cassius Crabb, found himself laughing aloud. He was so absorbed in the little show that his eyes didn't stray upwards to the discreet green-gloved hands pulling the strings until right at the very end, when the marionettes lay down to sleep and the crescent of children began to whoop and applaud. At this point, the curtains closed and an elderly man with wispy gray hair emerged from the side of the box, smiling broadly. He had prominent freckles on his face that almost gave him the appearance of a cheeky puppet himself.

'There's another show at noon for any folk what want it,' he announced. His voice was soft and low. He was well spoken and only slightly accented, possessing little of the broad Cornish brogue that had made Vickers so hard to follow.

As the crowds dispersed, Henry approached the man and extended his hand in introduction. 'Henry Herbert, Cassius Crabb Company.'

The man looked surprised and his eyes evaluated Henry. 'Pleased to meet you, Mr. Herbert,' he said. 'My name is Peter Tarny.' He removed his green gloves and firmly shook Henry's hand.

'I know your name, sir,' Henry smiled. 'Indeed, I know it well. If you will permit me to be frank, that is why I am here.'

Tarny looked genuinely confused.

'Your little theatre here is quite remarkable, sir. I represent Mr. Cassius Crabb and we would like very much for you to bring your show to the famous Paragon Theatre of Varieties.'

'I'm sorry, Mr. Herbert,' Tarny began, scratching his head. 'I don't know who or what you're talking about.'

'The Paragon Theatre is in London, sir. Cassius Crabb is

the finest purveyor of entertainment in the capital and he has personally selected you and your son's little theatre.' Henry grinned and turned up the showmanship. 'Imagine performing this show before a bustling crowd of a thousand fashionable Londoners, all cheering you on! Imagine your names on the playbills. Imagine the puppets you could make with this.'

With a sharp, sudden movement, Henry pulled a piece of paper from his pocket and thrust it into Tarny's hands. 'This is the monetary sum that the Cassius Crabb Company is willing to offer in return for a six week residency at the Paragon. Your travel costs and accommodation within the capital will also be provided.'

Peter Tarny stared at the sum on the paper with a look of near reverence. 'This is,' he paused and stammered a little, 'quite the surprise.'

'I have the full contract in my case here,' Henry continued. 'All you need to do is sign and the Company will take over from there.'

At this point, a younger man emerged from within the caravan. He shared some of the same features as Peter Tarny; the blue cat-like eyes, freckled cheeks, thick, full lips and wispy hair that flopped across his face, although the younger man's was a vivid blonde in hue.

'What's going on?' he demanded, seeing Peter's bewildered expression.

Henry smiled and began to speak, but Peter cut him off.

'Mr. Herbert, this is my son, Oliver.'

'Pleased to meet you,' Henry extended a hand. Oliver did not take it.

'What does he want?' Oliver was casting an evidently

suspicious eye over Henry's clothes and cane.

'He wants us to take our show to London,' Peter said, with a hint of astonishment in his voice. 'He wants to pay us to perform there.'

'Forget it,' snapped the younger Tarny. 'We don't need your money and we don't need London. We're happy here, thank you. Goodbye.'

'But, Mr. Tarny, sir,' pleaded Henry, 'I am making a very generous offer on behalf of my company.'

Peter showed Oliver the sum written on the piece of paper. Oliver ripped it in two and threw it on to the sand. 'Again, we don't need your money. We make enough here. Even with off-season coming up. People still donate. People still buy my marionettes. We're not struggling any more and we have come this far by ourselves. We don't need help from the likes of you.'

Henry chuckled, nervously. 'But, with respect, you don't even know what the likes of me are, Mr. Tarny. Besides, if I give you this money, you will still have earned it yourselves, through your talent and your reputation for fine entertainment.'

'Entertainment? Ha. You would never understand. Our home is here. Just leave us alone.' Oliver turned on his heel and disappeared back into the caravan.

'Wait, Oliver!' yelled Peter, following his son inside. 'Let us at least think about this!'

As the two Tarnys discussed the matter inside, Henry removed a cigarette from his tin case and casually smoked it, looking out at the sea and overhearing the occasional phrase of loud debate from inside.

'…thieves and liars…'

'…Oliver, please… your poor mother…'

'…don't you dare…'

'…make something of…'

'…lie in it!'

Eventually, Peter Tarny walked back out of the caravan, his head bowed. 'Please accept my apologies, Mr. Herbert. This must appear very poor hospitality after you've travelled all the way from London to see us. My son is a passionate young man and he has a lot of strong ideals, some of which I am very proud of; others not so.' He smiled. 'If you would accept my offer to stay with us here tonight in the caravan, then I am certain that Oliver and I can reach a decision by morning and let you know.'

'Thank you, sir,' replied Henry, tossing his cigarette away. 'Your hospitality is gracious and much appreciated. I look forward to hearing your views.'

As they entered the caravan, Henry was taken aback by its interior. Wall-mounted wooden shelves that housed a veritable army of marionettes obscured the walls of the main room. A small metal stove surrounded by mirrored tiles stood in the corner, away from the puppets. This clearly served to provide heating, lighting and cooking facilities, all in one. The floor was carpeted by worn maroon fabric and two velvet-covered seats sat in the middle of it. The puppets were the real draw of the room though. Henry had never seen so many of them. With their limbs all flopped over one another, it was difficult to make out what some of them were but there were little men, women, children, crocodiles, dogs and cats at least, all beautifully carved and bringing an almost blinding array of colours into the otherwise dark room. There were also several expertly mounted animals positioned on the floor and Henry felt a degree of nervousness as he passed by their glassy, lifeless stares. Taxidermy had always unsettled him.

A closed door led into another room, which Henry presumed must be the bedchamber. Oliver was nowhere to be seen.

'Make yourself at home. I'm afraid you'll have to push the chairs together and sleep in here tonight, but it should be warm at least,' said Peter.

'Thank you,' replied Henry, setting his case down on the floor and opening it to remove the contract. 'I'll leave this with the two of you. I think I may have a wander around the town whilst I'm here.'

'Of course. Thank you, Mr. Herbert. I must insist that you join us for supper at six though. It is the least I can give you for your troubles.' Peter smiled, gently.

※ ※ ※

Henry spent the day exploring the Polzeath sea front, admiring the views and browsing the shops that lined the promenade. He stopped in one gift shop and was charmed by a small wooden angel. The carving was notably fine. The angel's features looked slightly sad yet hopeful, her head lolling to the side, looking up towards God. Each feather on her wings was so clearly defined, and her painted green eyes seemed to shine, even in the gloom of the shop. He decided to purchase it as a gift for Sarah, to give to her upon his return.

'How much is this?' he asked the stumpy old lady behind the counter.

'Oi can sell you zat for a shilling, zir,' she replied, with a gummy smile.

He pulled out the coin and gave it to her, remarking, 'this is a very beautiful piece of work'.

'Indeed it be, zir,' she said. 'That be one of Oliver Tarny's. He zells a lot of 'is carvings to us an' they do well in zummer. He does 'iz puppet show on the beach, you know.'

Henry was surprised into silence by this odd coincidence, as the woman pointed to a mounted red setter dog sat on a cushion in the corner. 'That's Barston. Mr. Tarny stuffed 'im for me when 'e pazzzed on.' She made the sign of the cross over her chest.

'It's very lifelike,' observed Henry, trying not to be discomfited by the inanimate creature and its unblinking eyes.

When he left the gift shop, it didn't take him long to find the Crow's Nest, a rough and ready alehouse just off of the promenade whose greasy windows offered a pleasing view of the coast. He ordered a mug of hot spiced gin from the landlord and let it warm his hands from the slight chill in the air outside. Behind the counter, he couldn't help but notice a playbill from twenty years previous, adorned with cartoon-like figures and pretty script.

'PETER AND ANNIE TARNEY – THE LITTLEST THEATRE – POLZEATH PAVILLION'

Seeing the playbill and the carvings in the gift shop, he began to realise that the Tarnys were perhaps more closely tied to this quaint seaside community than he had imagined. For a moment he almost felt guilty for wanting to take them out of it. He snapped himself from this sentimentality and thought, with no small degree of envy, about how that bloody Oliver Tarny should be happy with his offer. He was being given a lot of money and an opportunity to enjoy the delights of the capital with it. He had been offered the limelight, something

Henry himself had never experienced and probably never would. A young, handsome, talented man like Tarny would go far in London. The sky would be the limit. How dare he throw all that away in the name of foolish pride and this sad pack of yokels?

Henry sat and stewed bitterly over his equally bitter spiced gin. A mounted parrot watched him through glass eyes from its perch. He didn't need to ask; he recognised this as Oliver Tarny's handiwork.

'You interested in puppets then?' asked the landlord, separating Henry from his thoughts.

'Hm? Oh. Yes. I'm interested in the Tarnys, actually. What they're doing there is quite remarkable. Probably the best puppetry I've seen.'

'Aye. I remember 'em from the days when it were Peter and Annie. When little Oliver were just sat in the audience.' The landlord leaned in, as though imparting a secret. 'That Oliver's an incredible young man now, mind. Even more talented than his parents.'

'What happened to Annie Tarny, if you don't mind my asking?'

'She died, sir, near twenty years ago now. She fell ill when Oliver were still a lad.' The landlord looked pensive, as he recounted his story. 'Took 'er a long time before she went. She were a stubborn little bugger. She wanted to stay around for 'er lad's sixth birthday. She died the day afterwards. Can't imagine it'd've been 'appy event, mind, what with 'er in the state she were in. Poor little sod, 'aving to watch that.'

'How very sad,' murmured Henry.

'Indeed, sir. She were much loved 'round these parts. I ain't never seen so many Polzeath folk in one place as there was at 'er funeral. Whole town came out to pay their respects and sing a few 'ymns.'

Henry mused on this story for a while as the landlord went to serve a local fisherman, who began conversing in impenetrable Cornish. He thought about his own mother's death and how few of the East End's inhabitants attended her funeral; a sombre, closed casket affair. Cassius Crabb had prevented Henry from seeing her towards the very end, at the peak of her suffering, so he had not endured what Oliver had. Crabb had also put Henry in employ immediately, running errands for him in between his intensive schooling, so the grieving process had been nipped in the bud by hard work. To this day, he still found death an uncomfortable subject to ponder, unaccustomed as he was to dealing with it. Now all these mounted bloody animals were everywhere, reminding him of its presence. He began to feel disorientated and left the alehouse, heading for the beach once more.

※ ※ ※

Dinner with the Tarnys was an awkward affair. They chewed a humble meal of liver and onions throughout which Oliver said nothing at all. Peter and Henry only just managed to sustain a steady stream of small talk about what it was like in the nation's capital. Henry lied through his teeth, naturally, painting his city as a golden paradise of glamour, success and happiness. Peter seemed suitably impressed and kept glancing at his son with a pleading, glazed look in his eyes.

Oliver retired immediately after dinner and Peter soon

followed, bidding Henry goodnight and leaving him alone in the main chamber. He turned the stove down low, so it now provided only rudimentary light and heat, pushed the chairs together and awkwardly sprawled himself across them, his damaged leg dangling over the side. He wrapped himself up in a blanket and went to sleep quite quickly. The gin from earlier and the heavy dinner had evidently eased his mind.

When he awoke it was still dark. He was uncertain of the time but it felt like the small hours of the morning already. His bad leg was aching tremendously, so he stood up to stretch and rub it. As his eyes grew accustomed to the low lighting, he focused on his surroundings and shivered. The glass eyes of the stuffed animals at his feet were shimmering in the dim glow from the stove. He looked upwards to avoid their stare and found himself equally unsettled by the shelves full of marionettes. The gaudy painted faces of the puppets seemed ugly and joyless in the gloom. Each with its glowing red cheeks and oversized wooden eyeballs looked like a grotesquely deformed caricature of the human form, miniaturised in some respects and enlarged in others. In the light of the Littlest Theatre, these exaggerations made the puppets amusing but lying lifeless, stacked upon one another like corpses in a plague pit, they became unnerving and bizarre. Their eyes seemed to stare blankly at him, challenging him to keep looking.

'Pull yourself together,' he whispered and reached out to touch one of the puppets, just to prove that it was harmless. He pulled a crocodile dressed in a faux-Elizabethan ruff from the shelf and, in doing this, dislodged some of the other puppets. There was a brief shuffling effect and it looked for a second as though they might fall. Henry reached out to push them back onto the shelf when, suddenly, a wide-eyed Jack Ketch puppet in full hangman's garb came tumbling down onto his face. He stopped himself from screaming aloud, but the stifled horror caused him to start gasping, as he tossed the puppet to the floor.

That looks like a sinister little man at the best of times, Henry thought to himself as he regained composure and smiled. The puppet's huge scowling eyes stared up at him from beneath its black cloth mask. He picked it up and put it back on the shelf next to the crocodile, deciding to take in some fresh air and calm down. He took his tin case of cigarettes and lit one as he stepped out of the caravan and into the windy night.

The sea was angry, its waves thrashing wildly against one another for as far as the eye could see. Henry rubbed his hands against the chill and felt a pang of longing for London. Polzeath had been pleasant for a few hours but now he missed the sound of people; the sound of life. A tap on his shoulder startled him.

'Evenin',' spoke a voice. It was Peter. 'Trouble sleeping?'

'A little, yes. I don't take to sleeping that well, I must admit, but I came out here because, uh…' He paused. 'I was a little unsettled. One of the puppets fell on me. I'm sorry if I woke you. I'm horribly embarrassed, to be honest.'

The old man smiled affectionately at Henry. 'Oh, don't be. Even Oliver used to be scared of the puppets when he was younger. When me and Annie used to put on shows at the Pavillion, I'd look out into the crowd and see Oliver with his hands over his eyes.' He chuckled. 'The only way I could stop him being afraid was showing him how I made them. We made our first puppet when he was only six years old, just after my Annie died. It was a little Mr. Punch that we built up from scratch. I carved the wood, Oliver helped fix in the joints and prepare the stringing. We made him a little outfit and a jester's motley. Annie used to make most of the costumes, so I was relieved to find that Oliver had such flair for it. We painted on the features together and I remember it was the first time the lad had laughed since the funeral. To be honest, it wasn't much of a Punch doll, as they go, but Oliver was so proud and happy; and he wasn't frightened of the puppets any more. Not once he knew he could control them and make them do what he wanted. Once he knew he was in charge. Spoilt little blighter, he was.'

'Well, I'm embarrassed and ashamed to be likened to a six year old boy, even one as obviously talented as your son, sir,' quipped Henry, twisting his weasel-like face into his best approximation of a charming smile.

Peter laughed. 'He never looked back once he overcame his fear. They've been his life ever since. Well, the puppets and the animals he mounts. The folk here almost always come to Oliver when a pet dies. These days with my stiff old limbs and achy fingers, I swear he's a better craftsman than I am.'

'Yes, I've seen some of his animals and carvings around Polzeath. They're quite astonishing.'

'I am very proud of him, Mr. Herbert. That's why I would so love to see him go to London and make something worthwhile of himself, not just rot away on the beach. It's bad enough I devoted my own life to this place. He's still young and I can't abide him doing the same.'

'Why doesn't he want to go?'

'He loves this place. He's told me he never wants to leave. He still goes and puts flowers on Annie's grave every week.'

'The residency in London is only for six weeks, initially…'

'Yes, but he's full of proud ideas that if we move to London, the puppets won't be his own any more. That he'll have to answer to one of the fat moneymen that he's read about in his penny dreadfuls. He sees London as a city of thieves and liars, to use his words.'

'That's absurd!'

'Perhaps so, but Oliver doesn't trust people very much at the best of times. Unless they're made of wood, that is. Then he knows they'll only do what's best for him, because he's the one pulling the strings.'

'It would be a pity if he did not know what was best for himself, then, and were to pull all the wrong strings.'

'Indeed.'

Both men smiled, wearily.

'I won't let him waste his talent, Mr. Herbert,' proclaimed Peter, a distinct certainty creeping into his voice. 'Both of us will sign your contract tomorrow morning before you leave. He doesn't have control over me. Much as he'd like to think he does, I am still his father.'

The two men looked at one another with a mild, but mutual, respect and walked back into the warmth of the caravan.

PART TWO : LONDON

Henry stood on the platform at Paddington station as the six thirty train from Bodmin pulled in, puffing out a plume of jet black smoke that rose to the arched roof and slowly evaporated. The air appeared tinted with a gray murk. The rank odours of coal, oil and smoke were thick enough to almost be tangible. Four weeks had passed since his return from Polzeath and this coming Friday would see the culmination of his efforts there. The Cassius Crabb Company had procured the Tarnys. Their residency at the Paragon was to begin in two nights' time. The transport had been arranged via telegram and, if all went according to plan – and Henry had made certain that it would do – the puppeteers and their props would be on this train.

Henry surveyed the busy platform, keeping an eye out for them. He saw Oliver first, heaving a large trunk from the carriage of the train and coughing, his blonde hair whipping about his face as he struggled. Henry limped over to assist.

'Mr. Tarny, sir, allow me,' he said, reaching for the trunk.

'It's quite alright, Mr. Herbert. I got it *on* the train myself. I'm certain I can get it off,' replied Oliver.

'Where's your father?' asked Henry, when the trunk finally rested on the platform.

'He is unable to join us. He has fallen ill and sends his apologies.'

'Ill, you say? Whatever's the matter?'

'It's nothing serious. A mere sickness of his stomach. I believe it was something he ate; he says it was a joint of meat from the Crow's Nest that they'd cooked bad.'

Henry's face fell. This was not what he had planned. 'So he will be coming on a later train? Tomorrow perhaps?'

'I doubt that. He told me that it would probably be next week at the earliest. He's always had problems with his digestion. The doctor told him to rest.'

'So,' Henry began, carefully, 'this means you will be performing your London debut alone?'

Oliver stared into Henry's eyes, as though to challenge him. 'Yes. It does.'

❖ DEBUT ❖

Henry tried smiling, but found it difficult under the circumstances. 'Oh, well, I imagine you are more than capable.'

Oliver let out a dramatic cough. 'Good God, this air is vile.'

'Come now, let's get a carriage to your new residence.'

Oliver began to lug the trunk across the platform. All of a sudden a man with a stooped back, dressed in mud-soaked rags, appeared by his side pulling at his cuffs. He looked up at Oliver. One of his eyes was plain white and appeared to be leaking fluid. His teeth were blackened nubs and, as he smiled, his gums were bleeding. His beard looked matted and sticky.

'Give you 'and, guv'?' he spluttered, hoarsely. A trail of blood and mucus dribbled from his mouth as he spoke.

'Dear God!' exclaimed Oliver in horror. 'Get this man away from me, Herbert!'

Henry pushed the beggar aside, and hit him lightly on the arm with his stick. 'Begone!' he snapped and the ragged man scuttled away to harass other passengers, clearly used to this type of reception.

The two men exited the station and Henry watched Oliver's face turn pale at the sight before him. The gaslights illuminated a busy West London street scene, although they were struggling to be seen through the yellow miasma of filth that stained the air. The smell was far worse outside the station than it was inside; a nostril-searing blend of horse manure, sewage and rotting fruit. The cobblestones were adorned with lumps of excreta; some dried, others still steaming and attracting flies. Henry was unresponsive to this everyday unpleasantness, but Oliver looked appalled.

Henry, secretly amused by his companion's horror, hailed a carriage for them to ride down the embankment towards Mile

End. As they boarded, and the driver helped the trunk up, the horse evacuated its bowels and nearly covered Oliver's shoes. He winced.

'Welcome to London!' Henry shouted, above the clatter of the carriage's wheels on the cobbles.

'This is disgusting!' Oliver appeared angry now.

'Your accommodation is in somewhat more pleasant surrounds,' began Henry. 'I have been instructed to settle you there tonight and make sure everything is as it should be. I can take your props over to the Paragon for…'

'No,' snarled Oliver. 'The puppets stay with me. They'd be stolen in minutes if I let them out of my sight in this place.'

'Oh, I'm sure that's not the…' Henry began but looked at Oliver's burning eyes and backed down. 'Fine. So be it. I understand you would want to be protective. In that case, I will pick you and your puppets up tomorrow morning at nine, then escort you to the Paragon. You will meet Mr. Crabb and begin rehearsals for the show on Friday. If you need anything, I am at your disposal.'

Oliver remained silent, denying Henry the pleasure of even a clipped 'thank you'.

'There has been much anticipation of your arrival here,' Henry continued, trying to raise some enthusiasm from his companion. 'Everyone is awaiting the debut London performance. Puppets are very popular in the music halls right now.'

Oliver turned his head to look out the window at the lumpy muck of the Thames, slowly floating by on the right hand side of the carriage. The fog was so thick that it was impossible to see across to the South bank of the river.

Henry surrendered the conversation and they passed the remainder of the journey in silence until they reached an inn, the Rose and Crown of Mile End. It was a shabby brick building squeezed awkwardly between an unmarked storefront and a quiet, cobbled side street. The two disembarked and Oliver retrieved his case while Henry tipped the coachman.

'This is where you will be staying. Mr. Crabb is a good friend of the proprietor and we can assure you will be most welcome and comfortable here.'

Oliver snorted, as they walked through the door and were struck by a cloud of tobacco smoke and a disjointed cacophony of sounds. A woman in a low-cut muslin dress played piano and sang 'My Old Dutch' loudly and off-key. Some drunk men gathered around her, singing along, groping the woman and sloshing their ale over themselves. A buzz of cockney yelling and shrieking female laughter bounced across each of the walls, punctuated with the occasional shattering of glass. Some eyes turned onto the newcomers, clearly struck by Oliver's unusual appearance. His pristine blonde hair, vivid blue eyes and crisp white shirt were not things one often saw in the Rose and Crown. There was a loud rustling of dresses and a ripple of excited giggles.

A dark-haired girl in a taffeta gown approached Oliver and ran her hand along his chin. ''Ello, my darlin',' she said, smiling at him. Her teeth were only slightly yellow. 'Buy us an 'ot mug of gin, would you?'

He recoiled from her touch. 'Please go away,' he said, his face turning crimson.

Henry smiled to himself. *The boy's a virgin*, he thought. 'I think you should go, Charlotte,' he said aloud to the girl, flashing a sly grin.

'Friend o' yours, 'enry?'

'No mere friend, Charlotte. He is the latest addition to the Cassius Crabb Company, my dear girl! If you want to know more, you'll just have to be at the Paragon on Friday to see what he's made of!' Henry gestured theatrically, pushed Charlotte aside and ushered Oliver towards a wooden staircase at the back of the room, trunk in tow. The whole room watched them with curiosity. This was excellent publicity.

At precisely nine o' clock the next morning, Henry escorted Oliver from the Rose and Crown. They walked the short distance to the Paragon Theatre of Varieties without speaking. A playbill adorned the front door and read *'By especial engagement: Tarny and Son's Littlest Theatre. Masterful magic from the far reaches of Cornwall!'*

As they made their way inside, a tall, smartly dressed man greeted them in the foyer. He had a showman's moustache and a square chin. His dark hair was sprinkled with flecks of gray and his eyes were such deep brown as to be almost black. His smile was broad but insincere as he greeted the two men.

'This is Oliver Tarny, sir,' announced Henry.

'Cassius Crabb,' the other bellowed. 'A pleasure to meet you, young Tarny. I have heard a good many things about you and your craftsmanship, so you had best not let me down.' His voice was deep and, although fairly well spoken, the grit of the streets occasionally scraped through into his accent. 'Where is your father?'

'He has been taken ill, I'm afraid, sir,' said Henry. 'Young

Mr. Tarny will be performing alone for the first week, until his father is well enough join him.'

'How unfortunate,' murmured Crabb, his mind visibly calculating. 'Is he capable?'

'I assure you I am more than capable, Mr. Crabb,' said Oliver, pointedly.

'Hmm. At least the audience doesn't see *you*, I suppose. As far as they're concerned, it's still Tarny and Son up there. It's the puppets they're here for.'

'Indeed.'

'Right you are. Let's get you into rehearsals.'

Crabb led the men into the main theatre. It was a good-sized auditorium and could accommodate one and a half thousand audience members on a good night. A central chandelier dominated the room. Oriental arches, draped in red velvet, stood between the stage and the seats. The walls were painted cream and pale blue, with gold relief. A cluster of ballerinas danced on the stage whilst a little man in glasses watched from the stalls, making notes in a journal.

'This is where we're going to make you a star, Tarny!' boomed Crabb, his voice reverberating through the room. 'Come and meet Mr. Bowler, the stage manager. He will provide you with what you need to rehearse today.'

The little man in the glasses stood up and evaluated Oliver as he greeted him. 'We've put you quite high up on the bill, just above the clog dancers. You had best not disappoint.'

'I assure you I won't.' Oliver spoke between gritted teeth. 'I was told my reputation preceded me.'

'Of course it does but this is London, lad, not Cornwall,' remarked Crabb. 'Now go on. Get your trunk unpacked and let's see what you can do.'

'I have one matter to raise first.' Oliver took a deep breath. 'Mr. Herbert, you said that you were at my disposal if I needed anything?'

'Absolutely.'

'Then I would like that you find me new lodgings. The Rose and Crown is ghastly. I could not sleep last night for the sound of the rats in the wall and those awful creatures downstairs in the lounge. You can't possibly expect me to perform well without good rest.'

'I see,' Crabb rubbed his jaw. He appeared annoyed. 'Henry, find the boy a better place. Tarny, you'd best be as good as you bloody say you are or you'll be sleeping in the bloody gutter come Monday.'

Henry was disappointed. He'd been looking forward to seeing Oliver's rehearsal and spending some time inside the theatre. It was a particularly foggy, acrid day outside. 'Yes, sir,' he muttered.

'And while you're out, pass a few bills around.'

Henry arranged for a room at the more expensive Ring O'Bells inn and spent an hour or two flitting between alehouses, posting up playbills for Friday's new line-up. He hated these mundane errands and cursed his employer for sending him out on them. When he returned to the Paragon, Oliver was nowhere to be seen, but Crabb approached Henry and shook his hand firmly.

'Henry, I have to hand it to you. I had no idea the boy was so talented. Well done. Well done for bringing him here. This performance is going to bring the house down.'

'I beg your pardon?'

◈ DEBUT ◈

'I just watched young Tarny rehearse. Astonishing stuff. The best puppet show I've ever seen in my life, I do believe, and I've seen some puppet shows! Never mind the father, this boy is gold! Herbert, if all goes well this weekend, I'm going to increase your wages for this. Maybe even a couple of pounds in your pocket for your efforts in Cornwall. I can feel this is going to be a phenomenon!'

Henry was dumbfounded. 'Thank you, sir. Thank you.'

A couple of pounds would go a long way for Henry. With the wage increase, he could break free even sooner from the confines of the Cassius Crabb Company, the Paragon Theatre and all the demeaning little errands associated with them. He couldn't wait to tell Sarah.

◈ ◈ ◈

On Friday night, the Paragon was almost shaking in its foundations from the activity of its clientele. Middle class gentlemen and ladies bustled their way in through the conservatory entrance towards the balconies. The lower classes clamoured and fought to get in downstairs and there was much drunken shouting between whores, barrel boys and fruit sellers, most of whom were familiar to Henry as he looked on from his place in Crabb's box.

Sarah Seabourne sat next to him, in a green velvet dress, white lace fichu and several silk ribbons. It was cheap and probably purchased second hand, but she wore it well. Her hair fell down across her bosom in curled nut-brown tresses. She looked beautiful to him in the soft glow of the chandelier and Henry took her hand, squeezing it gently.

'Mr. Crabb says he's giving me a higher salary if all goes well this weekend with the show,' he whispered in her ear. 'Because of my work in Polzeath.'

Sarah clasped his hand tighter. 'Oh! That's wonderful, Henry!'

He looked her in the eye. 'We're nearly there, Sarah. I've nearly enough for us to start thinking about, well, us.'

'You know I'll wait for you, darlin'.'

'I know. I just…'

Henry's words were cut off by the arrival of Cassius Crabb, accompanied by a noted Covent Garden prostitute. The pair of them sat down and Crabb gave Henry a firm pat on the back. 'This is going to be a night to remember,' he barked, laughing to himself.

A pianist began playing a jaunty melody as a troupe of clumsy ballerinas took to the stage. The act was of a sufficiently high quality to keep the audience in good spirits, so they cheered and shouted and sang along. A tightrope walker, a comedian, a bawdy female singer and some clog dancers all preceded Oliver Tarny's debut. The audience jeered good-naturedly throughout, then the comedian returned to the stage and began to talk. 'Right then, ladies and gentlemen! And the rest of yous! This next act comes all t'way from Cornwall and this is the first time they've performed in luvverly ol' London town! Please give a Paragon welcome to Tarny and Son!'

There was a round of raucous applause as the curtain behind the comedian lifted to reveal a blue sheet suspended from a rail in the centre of the stage. It measured around six by six feet. The audience were clearly confused by this and began to jeer. All of a sudden, a life-sized marionette, dressed in an untidy ruff, white shirt and patchwork trousers, flung itself over the sheet and collapsed onto the stage with a hollow thud. The audience shrieked with laughter.

'Told you this was good, Herbert,' Crabb said, nudging his assistant in the ribs. 'Very unconventional. Must've taken him bloody ages to make a puppet that size!'

Green gloved hands above the curtain pulled wildly at strings and the marionette sprang to life, waving its arms about. It began to dance in an uncoordinated manner, kicking its legs up high in time with the lively melody of the piano. The audience howled with joy, applauding and cheering the puppet on as it fell over repeatedly and smacked itself around the face. The puppet's arms and legs flopped up and down, slowly at first, then rapidly, as the audience howled and whooped. It wrapped its legs around its neck and spun gracelessly on its backside to great approval from the crowd.

'By Christ, that's bloody marvellous!' hooted Cassius Crabb, wiping tears of laughter from his eyes. He had clearly failed to notice that his assistant, beside him, was not laughing. Instead, Henry was staring at the stage with a look of ashen horror on his face.

The puppet's wispy gray hair obscured the face at first but Henry had soon recognised it and was now frozen with terror. The puppet's features were painted white with crimson circles on each cheek but the lips, although also tinted and distorted into a pained grimace, were thick and familiar. The eyes were large, deformed and made of wood, stuck inappropriately into their sockets and bulging out where once, Henry knew, they had been small and cat-like.

The marionette took a bow and left the stage. Henry snapped

back to his senses and leapt out of his chair. He knew he had to get backstage and find Oliver Tarny.

'What the deuce?' exclaimed Crabb, as his assistant bolted from the box. Sarah Seabourne looked equally baffled. The two of them stood up and attempted to follow Henry into the corridor, but he was running too fast, even with his bad leg, for them to keep up.

Henry nearly tumbled down the spiral stairs leading into the theatre's bowels and almost broke a ballerina's nose when he wrenched open the door to the backstage area, narrowly avoiding the poor girl's head. A sea of grease-painted faces looked up in alarm when he screamed, 'Where's Tarny? Where is he?'

No one said a word.

'Come on! One of you must have seen him! He was just out there!' He pointed wildly at the stage. He could still hear the roar of the crowd and the sound of a singing duo, but it was distorting in his ears to become an unpleasant buzz. 'WHERE IS HE?'

A dwarf in red jodhpurs signalled to a wooden door with a gold star painted on it and shrugged. 'Perhaps he's in there, Mr. 'erbert, sir. I think he went in there.'

Henry stormed through the bustle of performers, pushing them out of the way, barging towards the make-up room. A few of them huffed and tutted, as they attempted to clear a path for him.

He flung open the door with the star on it and looked into the room. There was no one inside and the large window at the back of it was open. Oliver Tarny's trunk sat in the middle of the floor, the giant marionette flopped inside it. Henry's hands shook with fear as he approached it. He reached out to touch the mannequin's face. It was unmistakably human skin, as he expected, dotted with freckles. There were thin cuts in the face where Oliver had sewn it onto its frame. The wisps of gray hair had been stuck on with glue. The giant wooden orbs that protruded from the eye sockets stared up vacantly with black painted pupils. He grabbed hold of the arms and pulled up the shirtsleeves, finding that thick wool puppet strings had been threaded deep into the skin. He snapped one of the fingers off. It was hollow and wooden beneath the skin.

In the puppet's mouth, Henry found a small card. On one side, the words, 'Tarny and Son's London Debut. October 16th, 1886' were written. On the reverse, it read, 'You Got What You Wanted'.

Henry turned around and vomited on the wooden floor. His whole body felt wracked with horror, revulsion and anger. Sarah Seabourne stood at the door, as Henry's juddering hands wiped sick from his whiskers and he stood to his feet.

'Henry? What on Earth is the matter?' she asked. 'Are you ill?'

'Get out of my way!' he roared, pushing her aside with some force.

'Henry!'

'GET OUT!'

He stormed past her in frustration and made towards the theatre's back door. He had to find Oliver Tarny. Cassius Crabb's large hands grabbed him and shook him. 'Pull yourself together! You're behaving like a madman! What is going on here, Herbert?'

'His... father...' rasped Henry, pointing to the make-up room and pulling loose from Crabb's grip.

He pushed open the back door and stumbled out into Mile End Road, still shaking. The fog was so thick, he could barely even see the drunken revellers in front of him, as they trod on his foot and staggered off into the darkness. He knew his chances of finding Tarny out here were remote. He could be halfway to Whitechapel by now. He was lost for good. Henry pushed the palms of his hands into his eyes in frustration.

The sound of the revellers grew distant.

'"You got what you wanted"', he whispered into the night. 'You bastard.'

The night swallowed his words and responded with grim, unbearable silence.

Clown Stations

·:¦:·

It was the big bosses who made the decision to carry freight for Clown Stations. Desperate times, they said. Apparently rail was uneconomical, inflexible. People didn't want to use it any more. But what would I know? I just drive the trains.

We all knew Clown Stations existed. We were briefed on their locations and were forbidden to stop there. Passenger trains sped up as they passed, so that no one onboard could catch more than a glimpse. Not that there was much to see. They looked like any other rural goods stations: just a small warehouse of corrugated steel and a platform. The only difference was the green rhomboid on the station sign with a black and white clown face painted on it.

I picked up my first Clown cargo at the terminus in the small hours, along with the rest of my freight. The large metal container was painted to look like a Christmas present. As I watched it being loaded, something felt wrong. I could hear sounds inside it. Rattling, gurgling, and something else. Tears? Or laughter? Whatever was inside, it was alive. The thought made me sick and nervous, and I felt worse as the four-hour journey continued. But what could I do? I kept driving.

I reached the Clown Station just before sunrise, shattering the morning silence with the screech of brakes. I watched from my cabin window as a man in a clown suit stepped out onto the station platform. At first I thought his giant blue eyes were real until I realised he'd painted them onto his eyelids. His real eyes, when they opened, were yellowish grey, without visible pupils. He glanced in my direction but I didn't think he could see me. His white greasepaint was streaky but his colourful costume resembled a kaleidoscopic beacon against the grey backdrop.

Three more clowns appeared, two dressed like the first and another in black and white stripes with a pointed hat. This one had dark eyes with tears painted down his cheeks, and he carried a crowbar. He approached the present-patterned cargo. The other three clowns tumbled across the platform and between them unfastened and unloaded it with startling efficiency. I stared in amazement; usually crates that big were moved only with a forklift.

The black and white clown prised off the sides of the box. Children sat inside, aged around three to six. They looked confused and frightened. Some sucked their thumbs. The four clowns began to dance, waving sausage-like white fingers in the children's faces and laughing hysterically. One tooted an air horn.

The black and white clown bared his teeth. They were long and sharpened to points. He moved closer towards a child as I frantically fired the train back to life and roared away from the platform, terrified of looking back.

It was the big bosses who made the decision to carry freight for Clown Stations. Desperate times, they said. Apparently rail was uneconomical, inflexible. People didn't want to use it any more. But what would I know? I just drive the trains.

Stop Press

⁂

Bernard Smith woke up on time, to the sound of the morning paper being delivered at 7 o'clock sharp. As was usually his routine, Bernard hopped out of bed, stretched a little and went into the hall to scan the headlines. He was dismayed however to find that instead of The Daily Mail, his paper of choice, the newsagent had pushed an unfamiliar publication through the door that morning. It was called The Daily Pry and looked frightfully dull by comparison.

Through still-bleary eyes, Bernard deemed the main story – CITY MAN WAKES UP ON TIME – to be uninteresting and filed a mental note to have stern words with his newsagent. Walking into the kitchen, he threw the tabloid away, filled up the kettle and took an apple from the fruit bowl. It was a particularly delicious apple and, as he savoured it with zeal, he decided it almost made up for the fact that he didn't get to read his chosen paper.

After pouring a cup of tea, Bernard returned to the hall only to find six more papers seemed to have been pushed through the letterbox. He picked up the unwanted pile and took a quick scan of the headlines, hoping that a copy of the Mail might be amongst them. No such luck. They were all copies of The Daily Pry. The front page on the top one read – KETTLE REACHES BOILING POINT, TEA TO FOLLOW – a curious headline to be sure. Its strangeness piqued his interest, so he read the accompanying article.

'City man Bernard Smith approached the kettle this morning and set it to boil,' it read. 'With intent to make tea, he stood and watched as the machine reached its limit. Controversy surrounds this move, with onlookers debating whether or not he was acting within the boundaries of the humane.'

Bernard stopped reading as the words registered. He decided this must either be a huge coincidence or some bizarre practical joke, so he flicked through the other five papers, reading the front page headlines.

PATEL LIVES IN FEAR: STERN WORDS PLANNED FROM SMITH – read one. Another read – PAPER MIX-UP MISERY. More alarmingly, the one at the bottom was headed – APPLE DELIGHT! 5 PAGE PHOTO SPREAD INSIDE! Bernard flipped it open and was horrified to find, indeed, a five-page photo spread of his eating an apple, including some rather unflattering close-ups.

Immediately he flung the door open, hoping to get a look at whoever was responsible for pushing these through the letterbox. As he looked down the hallway, a paperboy on a bicycle came hurtling up it shouting, 'Extra! Extra! Read all about it!'

Too surprised by the sight of a bicycle on a fifth floor hallway, Bernard stood dumbstruck as the paperboy launched a newspaper at his head. By the time he'd felt the impact and shouted, 'Oi! Get back here!' the boy had already turned the corner at the other end of the hallway and cycled out of sight. Bernard unfolded the paper that had hit him on the head and the front page headline glared mockingly: BERNARD'S BONCE BATTERED BY BOY ON BIKE!

Slightly scared, he hurried back into the flat and locked the door. The clock read 07:20, which meant that if he concerned himself much longer with this nonsense, he'd be late for work. He decided this was clearly some 'Candid Camera' style prank and that his boss would no doubt be unsympathetic about that sort of thing.

Pressing on, he walked to the bathroom and continued his daily routine as if nothing had happened. This involved shaving, using the toilet, taking a shower and dressing for work - nothing too exciting. When he returned to the hallway, however, it was now littered with what must have been around a hundred newspapers. He had trouble ploughing his way through them.

One headline in particular grabbed his attention as he kicked and tugged at the pile of papers – BERNARD SMITH: SHOWER SHOTS INSIDE!' He balked in shame at the accompanying blurred image of himself naked and drenched in soapsuds. A small star-shaped graphic labelled – EXCLUSIVE! – covered his modesty but left little to the imagination.

Bernard was aghast and decided there must be a hidden camera in the flat somewhere. Fighting his way across the sea of papers as yet more kept firing in through the letterbox, he eventually made it back to the kitchen, whereupon he began rifling through drawers and searching for the offending voyeuristic equipment. After several minutes without luck, he stormed back to the hall and saw the papers were multiplying at an incredible rate.

As he fought through the debris, now at least a foot high, a headline caught his eye and infuriated him yet more: SMITH STUMPED! SECRET SNAPPER REFUSES TO BE FOUND!

'Right! That's enough!' he bellowed and struggled to pull open the front door, angrily kicking away some of the papers blocking its path.

As soon as it opened he was confronted by not one, but a seemingly continual line of identical looking paperboys, all riding bicycles through the corridor and towards the flat! They each had bright ginger hair, prominent freckles, huge white smiles and a flat cap just like something from a 1940s cartoon strip.

'Hey! What on Earth is going on?' Bernard shouted to the first one in the line, but the boy ignored the question, instead tossing forth a paper with – SMITH : 'WHAT ON EARTH IS GOING ON?' – emblazoned across its front.

Bernard tried walking down the hallway corridor but the paperboys, despite the incessant ringing of their bicycle bells, seemed to be going out of their way to obstruct him. Out of breath and bruised slightly, he retreated into the flat, screaming 'Dear God!' at the top of his voice in sheer bewilderment.

As he closed the door and waded once more through the papers already inside, he noticed the new ones were bursting more quickly through the letterbox now and travelling a longer distance down the hall, almost like bullets from a gun.

He suddenly had a thought. 'What if I stand still?' he mused to myself and proceeded to do exactly that.

Silence.

The papers had stopped coming through the letterbox. Bernard remained motionless for what seemed like hours, but in reality was probably more like ten seconds. He breathed a sigh of relief. Had he at last put a stop to whatever was going on?

This optimism was shattered as a lone copy of The Daily Pry popped through the door. He carefully glanced down at the headline. SMITH STANDS STILL! HE THINKS IT'S ALL OVER! – it read. Bernard dropped to his knees and began howling in dismay.

'For God's sake!' he yelled at no one in particular. 'I just want to get to work on time! Is that too much to ask?'

Before he'd even finished his sentence, the papers began firing thick and fast once more through the letterbox. One of them struck Bernard between the eyes and knocked him to the ground. He struggled to get up and, each time he thought he was getting close to being vertical again, he was pushed once more to the floor by the force of a flying paper.

Within moments, the tabloids were covering Bernard's body and, the more he thrashed, the more they seemed to target whichever limb he flailed. He raised his head up and screamed for help, only to have a tightly rolled paper fly straight into his open mouth.

He began choking and, when he moved his arms in an attempt to remove the paper, they were knocked harshly out of the way by yet more of them, soaring through the air at a dangerous velocity. He was covered from head to toe in papers and struggling to breathe or move. As he gasped and wheezed one final time, he heard the sound of the last paper push its way through the letterbox. He didn't need to see it to guess what the headline read:

STIFF SMITH – DEATH RIDDLE OF NEWSPAPER CORPSE!

Emmeline

∴

Both of us are naked in this gloomy little room. I stand before the mirror. Grotesque, I cast a grim reflection of clumsy, lumpen masculinity. You lie around the room, still in pieces. Shreds of true beauty amongst the vile, pungent grime of our Hollow.

Of course, we remember this old place when it were still a deadlurk, before it got overrun by shirksters and dollymops and griddling dippers. Before it became this noisy hive of crooked humanity and hopeless dreams, unfulfilled and brushed away into the corners of its rooms, rotting among the dust and dead insects. I remember my own dreams that I brought with me to London. The dreams of our father, I should say. *The brute!* A cloth bag of underwear, a hand-me-down suit and a pair of thick'uns for me to get started in an apprenticeship. That was what he gave me, as much his foundation for my future as it was his penance for the demolition of my childhood.

It wasn't until I met you that I discovered myself again. Memories of sunny afternoons dressing up and playing outdoors. This new feeling of being free and not afraid of my own shadow in the evening gaslight. No longer watching it, fretfully expecting its tenebrous hands to spring out and choke the miserable life from me. *O, how I love you so much more than myself.* We're older and London has changed so much since then, yet still I feel incomplete unless you're there. Awkward and displaced.

Now in this filthy hole, worth its tuppenny rent only as a means of avoiding the crushers, I scrape the razor one more time along my face and begin bringing you back to life.

I start with your corset, the ragged old whalebone bought with our father's sovereigns. I slip it onto your body and tighten each lace, carefully moulding the shapeless meat into something feminine, something perfect. I awkwardly guide your legs - never your most handsome feature - into a muslin underskirt. Nothing underneath. Anything else will only be a burden later for the dark duties of your night work.

Your finest dress of satin and blue tinsel is draped across the splintering wooden crates I made into our bed. It glitters in the glow of the spirit lamp. As I fasten you into the dress, you show signs of life once more. I use a pair of old greasy rags from the basement boiler room to fraudulently stuff the dress, accentuating your paltry chest, reaffirming the femininity that whispers *'touch me'* in the murk of the alleys at square-rigged gentlemen with Newgate knockers and fine Chesterfield coats.

Finally, I paint your face with a delicate artistry I am capable of only with you, forcing out those exquisite bright eyes - no longer the milky, murky pools so morbidly reminiscent of the blood and spend you've seen too many times dripping into the rainy gutters of the Seven Dials. Yes, just a touch of bismuth, a pinch of belladonna and a little beetroot juice on your lips create a *belle* from what was mere limpid flesh.

I take your hair from under the bed and gently position it on the balding scalp, covering patchy tufts of mousy brown with rolling crimson tresses. I tie a green silk dobbin around it as the final touch and you come to life in all your soft-lit glory. A glimmering Goddess in the sooty black sickness of our room.

I look in the mirror now and see your reflection. True elegance before me. No mere old molly. I see the Queen of the Penny Gaff. Sweet perfection. *Emmeline…*

Come Die With Me

·:::·

The world was a far lonelier place before the internet, Martin reckoned. Online social networking had brightened the dark, friendless existence of the nervous, shy or socially awkward worldwide but, more importantly, it had made bonding easier for those like Martin. People whose leisure interests leaned away from the mainstream, toppled towards the esoteric and plunged downwards into the outright bizarre.

Martin enjoyed the abduction and strangulation of schoolgirls between ages 13 and 16, although he also dabbled in privately modelling their clothes, cooking and eating their flesh and meticulously arranging their boiled, polished skulls in his Trophy Chamber. Finding friends who might also embrace these obsessions seemed like a long shot and Martin, a perennial loner, had all but given up on the idea. His job as a sewer flusher kept him either busy or tired much of the time and he had his girls for company at home whenever the mood took him.

He occasionally used the internet for pornography but, of late, had been feeling that even the most depraved and illegal sites he could find were unsatisfactory and frustrating. This failure of his body to fulfil the needs of his mind was what led him to an online health forum relating to erectile dysfunction. Within days of signing up and posting a vague explanation of his situation, he received a friendly private message from a user called bluevanman1969. This was Tony, a local bloke who'd been born and bred in the East End of London and had spotted Martin's Walthamstow location on his profile. Tony thought that, being two men of a similar age and locale, they should go for a drink to discuss their respective issues with impotence. Martin was wary to begin with but soon agreed mostly out of a need to distract himself from the existential despair that had overcome him since his most recent kill; a wholly drab, unexciting experience.

Surprisingly, the two men hit it off instantly and Martin, never usually one to enjoy the company of the living, found himself wanting to spend a lot more time with Tony. They began meeting several times a week in the Helen Of Troy, where they'd drink beer, chew the fat of their respective problems, bang on about what they'd change in the world if they were its rulers and lament over the Leyton Orient result. Man talk, basically.

After a month or so, Tony took Martin back to his flat and said that, if their friendship were to progress, he would have to be honest with him. With an absence of dramatic flair, Tony confessed to being a serial killer. Mostly stabbing and mostly male victims in their 20s and 30s. He said the thrill of snuffing the life out of strong, young, healthy men was unbeatable. For a second Martin worried that Tony would kill him – although he was hardly young or strong – but apparently this was not the reason for the sudden confession. Instead, Tony just said he'd seen something in Martin's eyes that made him think he could admit to this and not be judged.

Tony had been right, of course. Martin felt a sense of relief like no other as he poured his heart out to his new best friend and confessed that he, too, had killed and would kill again. The pair embraced, cried a little and drank whiskey until the early hours, recounting their finest slaughters to one another with much laughter and a sense of mutual admiration.

In the morning, over a fried breakfast at a café on the High Street, Tony told Martin in whispers about a small club of fellow killers who had been meeting for a while with the aim of adding some spice and social interaction to their traditionally solitary hobby. When he asked if Martin was interested in joining, the answer was an emphatic 'yes!'

Over the course of a few weeks, Martin was introduced to the other three members and became accustomed to the way they operated. Contrary to his belief that serial killers were low on humour – based as much on his own personality as anything else – they all seemed convivial, upbeat and even mischievous folk.

Maria was the most outwardly crazy and unnerved Martin a little with her raucous laughter and flamboyant personality. At 25, she was also the youngest of the group; a slim, outgoing Spanish nurse with a penchant for killing the elderly, middle-aged or disabled. She had no method of choice, instead finding that variety kept things fun.

Diana was a much older and more voluptuous lady from Hampstead who worked as a teacher at a private school there. When her stockbroker husband was away on business trips, Diana killed young men she picked up at bars throughout the country. A drop of poison in their martinis usually made for a slow, lingering death that Diana enjoyed watching while pleasuring herself.

The remaining member of the group was Benjamin – a tall Jewish gentleman in his mid-30s whose speciality was families. As a semi-celebrated historian, Benjamin held an interest in genealogy and believed he could make or break history by decimating family lines. He also had a gleeful sadistic side that made the rest of the group look like philanthropists.

For some years now, the club had entertained itself with various games and challenges that both appealed to the individual members' fetishes and collectively nurtured a sense of shared enjoyment. Tony told Martin that this was just what he needed to put some lead in his pencil and be able to once more enjoy murder. Martin, already high on just being able to open up and talk about his murders at last, was certain that Tony was right.

As a group, they hatched the idea of a game called 'Come Die With Me', loosely based on a similarly named TV game show. The rules of the show were that five strangers would host dinner parties for one another and give each other scores for the quality of both the food and the company. The murderous twist that the club added was that each member would indeed hold a party but the meal would be replaced with a murder.

Martin felt that the game got off to a flying start over at Benjamin's house. It had been decided that to increase everyone's participation, the guests would supply the victim or victims as a gift for the host. Diana had chosen Jake Barstow, a single father of two daughters who both attended her school in Hampstead.

On the day of the dinner party, Maria went to the Barstow house in the guise of a charity worker and had worn a skirt short enough to sufficiently distract him while Martin broke into the back of the house and abducted the two girls. On the signal, Maria chloroformed Barstow and they all piled into Tony's blue transit van which was parked nearby and ready for a quick getaway.

It was the most excited Martin had felt in months and accomplishing the abduction with friends instead of by himself made his heart swell with pride at how well he'd handled it and also with the simple joy of sharing.

Upon arrival at Benjamin's, Martin had been awe-struck by the man's innovative and exciting treatment of the victims. Ben graciously thanked the rest of the club for supplying such a fine gift and, as everyone took their seats in the living room, began his work. He swiftly disembowelled Barstow with a hunting knife and then, in a stroke of genius, tied the two screaming girls together with a long loop of their father's intestinal tract. After several hours of verbally abusing them and smearing them with blood, he made them push their heads together and then shot them both through the skull with a single golden bullet. Martin couldn't help himself and applauded loudly as they hit the ground. He gave Benjamin a perfect 10 out of 10 mark for the evening that, in his eyes, had been a delight from start to finish. The others were impressed but had not been quite so generous. Even so, Benjamin had scored a presentable 29 points in total.

This week, however, it was Martin's turn and the excitement had been overtaken by nervousness. He really wanted to impress his new friends – to show them what he was capable of – but agonised over how to better Benjamin's effort. After several sleepless nights of wondering both what the victim would be like and what he was going to do to her, he settled on an elaborate choking technique involving a complex arrangement of ropes that he'd seen on a Japanese porn website.

Tony was the first guest to show up on the evening and he put Martin's nerves to rest by providing two fine 16 year olds. One was a bottle of single malt and the other a semi-conscious girl in a school uniform with a cloth bag, covering her head and her hands and feet tied together by string. It made Martin's pulse quicken and he licked his dry, cracked lips in anticipation.

Diana showed up next and brought with her a tub of rock cakes that she had baked herself. She air kissed Martin and said she was really looking forward to the evening and just knew he could do it. Benjamin was next and looked a little flustered. He was supposed to give Maria a lift but, in his excitement, had completely forgotten and left her at home. Embarrassed, he explained that he'd called her and offered to pay for a taxi but she claimed she wasn't feeling well anyway and would just have to make it next time. Although she'd sent apologies, Martin was a little sad that she couldn't be there to see his inaugural kill. Even so, he was determined not to let this ruin the night. At least the others were there.

As they all poured drinks and toasted one another, Martin took them into his Trophy Chamber and talked them through a potted history of his career as a murderer, starting with the juvenile souvenirs of his early years – underwear, hairbands, tubes of lipstick – before moving onto his amateur photography and, finally, the skull collection. The skulls – freshly polished that morning – certainly drew some impressed sounding 'oohs' and 'aahs' and, as they walked back towards the bedroom where Martin's rope apparatus was set up, he felt a stirring beneath the waist that had been missing for a very long time.

The schoolgirl was on the floor, trying to untie herself and escape when they returned. Martin grabbed her – perhaps more forcefully than he usually would, in the interest of theatrics – and pushed her onto the bed. He yanked the cloth bag from her head, anxious to see the fear in her eyes, and was about to announce his intentions when he looked down and saw that there, beneath him, in the school uniform was Maria. She'd bitten her lip and a ribbon of blood trickled from her mouth but she was laughing.

Before Martin had chance to ask any questions, Maria had slipped her hands free of the rope and pulled a knife from inside her school blazer. She pushed it into Martin's throat and slit all the way across, squinting as the blood sprayed into her face from his main artery. Her drenched, red grimace – eyes closed, mouth locked in malicious joy – was the last thing Martin saw as he collapsed lifeless on top of her, rattling and gurgling like a sick, helpless infant.

Benjamin, although nearly doubled over with laughter, managed to haul Martin's twitching, bleeding corpse off of Maria and all four remaining club members chuckled about the mess and applauded one another's effort. As Tony poured them each another glass of Scotch, it was unanimous that Maria's party had been the best one yet. Perfect 10s all round.

Lambkin

·:⁘:·

The layout of Paddington station almost entices you to venture further than you'd planned. Sometimes even further than you could imagine existed.

When changing underground lines from the Bakerloo to the Hammersmith & City, you must first come up from the tunnels and walk almost the entire breadth of the station. This means, on the dreary shuffle between one dark, grubby tube to another, you pass all the luxurious first-class compartments on warm, comfy-looking trains bound for obscure locations in the Southwest of England. I've often made this trek and wondered how many other bored commuters, feeling trapped by the rigid rush-hour regime, have contemplated just hopping one of these trains and seeing how far away it takes them.

It was around 6pm, some random evening in April, when I decided to test this for myself. I was on my way to a Monday evening shift and felt an incredible urge to escape, to get away; not just from work, but from the shackles of London itself for a while. Also, more importantly, from Billie, who had been particularly insufferable that day.

I had moved in with Billie Rutherford at the start of my second year at London Met. I responded to her Flatshare Wanted ad on the board of the Student Union bar. She was living in a nice but tiny two-bedroom place in King's Cross and was on the verge of desertion by her flatmate who was dropping out of Uni altogether. I, meanwhile, had grown tired of sharing a grim, shabby old terrace off Seven Sisters Road with five other people and, with the money I was making through part-time bar work, could at last afford the step up.

We hadn't met prior to my showing up at the flat - I was studying History and she Child Psychology - but we hit it off fairly well and I liked the place enough to offer up a month's rent in advance. The deal was sealed. With both of us scurrying in and out all the time to lectures, seminars and part-time jobs, we saw each other for only a few hours a week yet still we bonded through our respective stresses, usually shared over takeaway pizza on Friday nights or several drinks at the Union bar on the weekend. In short, we became good friends. I usually keep myself to myself and clam up in social situations, so it was nice to have someone around whom I could feel comfortable.

It all went wrong when September came and we decided to renew the twelve-month lease on the flat even though Uni was over. Both of us had gained our degrees but were at a loss with what to do with our lives. I decided to stay on in London, purely through a lack of anywhere else to go. The thought of returning home to Sheffield and my parents felt like a dead end. Although I'd never really settled in London, I'd managed to secure some low-paid work as a research assistant for my History professor in the day and this, coupled with the bar work I was still doing several nights a week, meant I could comfortably pay my way.

Billie, on the other hand, was struggling. She just about made ends meet with the occasional babysitting job, but mostly spent her time applying for permanent positions and failing to even get interviewed. Over the last winter, the job applications seem to get fewer, while the hours she spent playing online games and eating baklava from the deli underneath our flat seemed to be forever increasing. The sticky grease paper from the sweets began to litter the kitchen, living room and even hallway of the flat. By around mid-January our lives had split off in such different directions that we barely spoke and when we did, there was usually tension. My life focused on work; hers on avoiding it.

Before I headed off to Paddington and to work, that night in April, I had been enjoying a rare free day. No work at the university meant a chance to tidy the flat and catch up on some history periodicals that I seldom had time to read. However, Billie had stormed into my room sometime in the afternoon and demanded we had a talk. She levelled a good many accusations at me, ranting that I was selfish and a terrible friend.

'You never even ask how the job search is going any more,' she spat at me with a look of disdain. I didn't like to say that this was because I sincerely doubted she spent more than a few minutes a week actually searching for jobs, so remained silent as the charges continued. 'You're so wrapped up in your stupid research job and your bloody history papers, you don't even stop to say good morning. It's like I don't even exist for you any more.'

She was right. Communication within the flat had broken down. Without the bond of academia to tie us together, we ultimately had little to talk about and with all the time I was working, it was hard to muster up the energy for small talk at the end of the day. I tried feebly to explain this but it all came out wrong and, in the end, I agreed that we would spend at least one night a week together, just chatting like we used to. I felt like I was being bullied into it and strongly suspected she had picked up the one-night-a-week idea from some kind of internet self-help page; still, I played along to keep the peace.

I felt my temper beginning to flare so I decided it would be best if I got out of her way for the night before things worsened. We still had at least eight months together left on the lease, so the last thing I needed was to make the atmosphere unbearable. I left the flat a little early for my shift at the bar, after taking care to inform Billie of my whereabouts and even ask, 'how's the job search going?'

'Pretty shit, if you must know,' she replied, resignedly.

After I'd settled on the train and unconvincingly called in sick to work, I continued fuming over the whole thing. It was almost as if she were trying to force a friendship upon me when there was barely one there, yet I knew that fighting against it would only make things intolerable within the flat for the rest of the year. The ticket inspector interrupted my thoughts.

'Can I see your ticket, sir?'

'Oh, I'm sorry, I didn't have time to get one at the station or I'd have missed the train,' I replied, my hands open toward him in apology.

He seemed to believe me and sold me one there and then. I asked for a single ticket all the way, deciding I would just hop off whenever it felt right. When he printed the ticket, I examined it and saw that the train's apparent terminus was Exeter. I'd never been further west than Hammersmith before.

I dozed off for about an hour, after staring out of the window at the buildings going by and the sun setting. When I woke,

I stretched my arms and saw that the buildings had turned into trees and the sky was now almost black.

The train slowed to a halt and, pressing my eyes against the window, I could just about make out the grimy old sign on the station wall – 'LANGFORD'. The platform was empty. A wooden gate at the end of it was marked 'EXIT'. The ticket office looked closed. A rusty street lamp loomed, burnt-out and broken, whilst a phrase - 'Permit To Travel' - glowed menacingly from the decrepit ticket machine that offered a sole light in the darkness. This seemed a suitable contrast to London, so I alighted, feeling a strange sense of adventure well up inside me.

The air had taken on a faint chill, but I didn't let this bother me. Wrapping my coat tighter around me, I made my way through the wooden gate and on to a fairly well lit residential street. Terraced houses lined each side of the road and a convenient sign in front of me pointed towards the town centre.

It was a brisk ten-minute walk before I found a row of shops that I assumed was the high street. It was already after closing time, so most of the storefronts were blanked by metal shutters or just panes of dull glass, reflecting my image in the unlit murk of their interiors. The shops themselves were similar to what you'd find in any high street. I don't know quite what I was expecting but I couldn't help feeling disheartened when confronted with the perennial chain store signs with their logos identical to those of their counterparts in London. The entire street was pretty much interchangeable with any other in my experience of suburban England. I decided a drink was in order.

The first pub I saw was a homely looking place called the Eagle Vaults. The building itself appeared to be 19th century and, although it looked fairly quiet, I decided to nip in for a quick pint. Again, I found myself disheartened that all the beers on tap were from major breweries. I was hoping to sample one of the local ales, but in their absence, contented myself with a pint of John Smith and a game pie from the chalkboard menu.

The pie took half an hour, or three fast and nervous pints, to arrive. It was stringy and tasted of old socks. When I'd worked my way through it and looked out of the window, I noticed it had started to rain somewhat whilst I'd been eating. My heart sank and I realised that whatever stupid ideas I'd had about getting out of London and relaxing in some idyllic countryside paradise were certainly not going to be fulfilled here. The only upside was that my mind had been taken off my fight with Billie for an hour or two.

I sighed and decided to cut my losses.

'Can I get a taxi to the station?' I asked the barman.

He was young and friendly enough. He smiled at me and said, 'Well you can, but I don't know what for. The trains have all stopped runnin' for the night, so they 'ave.'

'I beg your pardon?' I asked, incredulously.

'The last train out of Langford goes at eight o'clock. You just missed it.'

When he realised he had rendered me speechless, he rummaged under the bar and pulled out a yellowing, dog-eared train timetable. Sure enough, the pamphlet confirmed, the last train out of Langford leaves at eight.

'If I'd known you was plannin' on takin' it, I'd've told you earlier, I would.'

'I wasn't expecting that,' I announced pathetically, my eyes falling to my shoes.

The barman smiled again and asked if I would like the number of a decent Bed and Breakfast. I accepted his offer and, within ten minutes, was in a taxi bound for the Wycombe Lodge, a small, grotty-looking guesthouse, run by a middle-aged man with a lazy eye, a lopsided hairpiece and a heavy West Country accent. Through a combination of his accent and my desperation to just go to sleep and forget the whole thing ever happened, I barely caught what he said as he ran through a list of house rules. I just smiled as politely as I could and took the room key from him.

As I lay on the loud, springy bed and stared up past the brown wallpaper to the yellowed roof, I realised I had never felt so sad or directionless. I started crying quietly, wondering what I was going to do and what my plan was for the rest of my life. I had fled Sheffield to get away from my parents and my fear of turning out like them. I had leapt into the cold embrace of the biggest, busiest city I could imagine and had found nothing there for me. I had gained my qualification and was once more without ties and feeling the wanderlust. I was longing for some peace and quiet and yet part of me suspected I would find neither wherever I went. I hated the bar work, the research job felt like it was going nowhere and I was even beginning to hate my only real friend. I was lost. To make it worse, I'd just spent £35 on a hideous room at a B&B in the middle of nowhere. I felt so stupid and wrong that I cried myself to sleep for the first time in years.

By the time I had woken up and looked at my watch, it was 8am and already bright outside. I pulled back the faded paisley curtains of the room and looked outside at the street below. My eyes were a little sore and dry but, otherwise, I felt significantly better than I had done the night before. The light shining through the window seemed to fill me with a nebulous hope. The smell of bacon and eggs sizzling downstairs filtered through the gap beneath the room door, making me happily hungry. I splashed some water on my face and enjoyed the uncommon treat of a full English breakfast.

As I checked out and stepped onto the high street, I realised Langford looked different in the daytime. A kind-faced old man walked past with his dog and wished me a good morning. I nodded and smiled to him in return, deciding to take a stroll myself and see where it would lead.

It wasn't long before I'd walked past the station and was heading away from Langford altogether, admiring the burgeoning blossom that lined trees along increasingly narrow roads. I soon veered away from these and down a bridle path. This ran beside a grassy field and past a sign that read 'Lower Langford'. I climbed the first of many crooked stiles and continued to stroll, the sun radiating warmth on me, the morning chill now dissipated altogether. When I looked at my watch, an hour and a half had passed and the next sign I saw was a barely noticeable one that read 'Welcome to Wickstow' on a chipped whitewood board.

Aside from a few pretty thatched roof cottages that dotted the streets, Wickstow seemed to offer very little to the casual visitor. A stooping Tudor-style pub, The Bear's Head, stood next to the village green. Some other white-fronted buildings bore signs promoting their commodities. I stopped into the newsagent and bought a cold can of Pepsi from the red-faced old lady inside. The sugar and caffeine perked me up and I ambled towards a wood on the outskirts of the village. There were small, immaculately rounded hills in the near distance and I decided to head towards them. This was turning into a full-scale nature ramble and I was definitely enjoying the experience.

It was behind a low tangle of bracken and heather that I spotted the unusual stone structure. I had strayed a little from the main dirt track and was in a darkened area of the woods where the huge oak trees dominated the sky, forcing the sun to almost back away. My curiosity piqued, I clawed my way through the bracken, was stung by nettles for my troubles and eventually saw that behind the undergrowth, there indeed lay a small and, by the looks of it, very old little house made of stone.

There was only one floor to the house and it couldn't have been more than about ten foot wide. I had trouble placing the date, but it certainly looked rickety and dilapidated enough to have been there a fair while. The front door was made of wood and was covered with tiny holes, where it had been partially eaten away by woodworm. Above the door was a large stone plate with the word 'Lambkin' crudely carved into it. On the grounds that any bolts or locks that may have been present had long since eroded or been stolen, I cautiously let myself in.

The house had clearly not been inhabited for some time. There were no modern furnishings, no sign of electricity or gas or even windows. The floor was made of cold stone, overgrown with moss and mould. Huge and elaborate spider webs hung from each corner of the room. With the sun just about shining through the door, I could make out the remains of a fireplace – now just a soot pile – in the corner of the first room. A rusted copper kettle lay nearby. There was an arched doorway leading into a second, far smaller room and I used my cigarette lighter to get a better view of what was within. It was almost as if this annex had been added as an afterthought. There was a different kind of stone on the walls and I would've taken a guess that this room had been there, in some form or other, even longer than the larger one. The floor inside it was made of wood and the floorboards creaked and bent as I tentatively put my weight on them. Creeping over to the edge of the room, I noticed something bizarre on the floor and bent down to take a look.

It was a bent pair of dusty, black-rimmed NHS spectacles with the lenses removed. I smiled, slightly perplexed, and held them up before me. Just then, I heard the sound of a dog barking nearby which startled me so much that I lost my balance and fell head first on to the floor. I put my hand forward in an attempt to land safely and cursed as it went cracking through the rotten floorboard and down into the wormy earth below. Gasping, I pulled my hand out and brushed it against my trouser leg in a vain effort to clean it up. When I'd recovered from the shock, I laughed uneasily to myself and bent down once more to check with my lighter if anything was hidden under the boards.

In amongst the dust and soil, there definitely seemed to be something. I put my hand back in with some reluctance and scraped around, eventually pulling out a small metal object. Getting irritated by the lack of light in the small room, I returned to the larger chamber and examined my find by the light of the sun shining through the door. It was some kind of wax sealing device. A cylinder, about six inches long with a design carved into the bottom. The design itself was quite bizarre and as tricky to date as the house itself. It had a large, snaking letter L in the middle, flanked by crude images of a mallet on the left and a chisel on the right. In the clear absence of anyone around to claim ownership, I slipped the seal into my pocket and decided to investigate further when I got back to London.

It was only just after midday by this stage and I didn't have to be back at work until half-seven that evening, so I stopped by the village pub for a pint and some lunch. I was hungry after all the walking I'd done and in a good mood, having found something unusual and possibly of historical interest to get my teeth into.

The Bear's Head was pleasant and well lit, with ancient wooden beams adorning the ceiling and a slew of large wooden tables. A few men in Barbour jackets were congregated at a table in the middle and a couple of solitary drinkers sat in shaded corners. An extensive menu board adorned the wall near the bar and behind it stood a large man with pork-chop sideburns and stubble, next to a young brunette of about sixteen or seventeen, whom I guessed must've been his daughter.

'Good day to you, squire,' he said, unfolding his arms and resting them on the taps. His voice was soft, inflected by the West Country accent, but not impenetrably so.

'Good day. Pie of the day and a pint, please!' I smiled and pointed to one of the ale taps.

He began to pour a glass of cloudy local brew, as the young

girl scuttled away to the kitchen out the back. 'You come 'ere to see the castle, did you?'

I looked blank. 'Castle?'

'Aye, Langford Castle. That's what brings most folk here, not that we really get much in the way of visitors.'

'I didn't know there was a castle, to be perfectly honest. I just started walking and, err, well, arrived here.' I felt strangely embarrassed by this confession. 'Where is it?'

'Well, there's not much left now. It's a ruin up on the hills. You can just about see it from the village. It was built in the 17th Century. Not a lot to see, to be honest and it's been neglected for years. Just gets more and more run down, mind.'

'That's interesting.' I thought I'd try my luck. 'Do you know anything about the little stone cottage in the woods back that way?'

The landlord's face darkened like something out of a horror film. 'You don't want to be going near there,' he said. 'Bloody place is a death trap. Dunno why they 'aven't torn it down already. Bits of stone and wood 'anging orf everywhere, mind.'

'Any idea how old it is? Or why it's there?'

'Can't say as I do. Don't know much about it at all, to be honest. I'd steer well clear if I were you.'

I felt like giggling at the man, he seemed to be taking it all so seriously but I managed to compose myself enough to thank him, lift my glass and take a seat at a nearby table while he served another customer.

The ale was excellent and, before long, the girl came out to place a golden-crusted pie on my table.

'You was asking about the cottage then?' she asked, brazenly taking a seat opposite me.

'Err, yes, I was,' I replied, taken aback by her forwardness.

'Don't listen to my dad, he's just a superstitious ol' sod. The place is haunted apparently, so the story goes.'

'Haunted?'

'Yeah. Beware of the boogeyman, and all that. We used to dare each other to go in. None of us ever really got past the front door. It's pretty scary. We were always 'you go in', 'no, you', 'I dared you first', 'bugger orf', y'know?'

'Don't suppose you know how long it's been there or what it was built for?'

She snorted, a little derisively. 'No way. It's been there for buggerin' ages, I ain't got a clue. Specky Russell spent the night there once. He was running away from Billy Thomas and his gang and didn't know anywhere else to hide. Specky were never the same after that. He wouldn't tell anyone what 'appened but he lost his glasses in there so his mum gave him a right ol' hidin'. They 'ad him sent to an 'ome in the end. He went nuts.' With this, she put her finger to her forehead and spun it around, just for emphasis.

I laughed. 'That's a good story. You must tell it to all the tourists.'

'Bugger orf,' she said, half-jokingly flipping me the V sign. 'I just wanted to know why you were interested, that's all.'

'I'm a history scholar. I saw the cottage while walking and I was curious. It's quite an unusual little building to just be standing there, forgotten about in the woods.'

She shrugged. 'I guess.'

Her father finished serving a big-eared old man in a knitted jumper and barked across the room. 'Hey, you. Them pies won't cook 'emselves, you know!'

'Yeah, yeah,' she murmured, getting up and rolling her eyes at me. 'Daft old sod.'

'Thanks for the info,' I said, with a light hint of sarcasm.

I was back in London by six that evening and popped back to the flat for a shower and a change of clothes before work. Wrapped in a large bath towel, I returned to my bedroom to find Billie sat there on the bed, looking angry and impatient.

'Excuse me?' I asked in response to her glare.

'Where the Hell have you been?' she growled.

'I've been out. Does it matter?'

'It would've been nice of you to tell me.'

'I didn't realise I was going myself until I got there.' I muttered, fumbling around in my drawer for a shirt and some pants. There was a drawn-out silence.

'Have you got a girlfriend, is that it?' she asked. I turned around to face her and suddenly saw the strangest look in her eyes. Her recent behaviour started making sense. Billie had feelings for me. No wonder she had become so possessive. I felt an immense crushing feeling in my heart and was rendered speechless. I suddenly felt giddy, like I was unable to handle this and things between us were spiralling out of control.

'Well?' she asked, her voice cracking a little with ill-concealed desperation.

'No,' I replied, my head bowed a little. 'No, I haven't got a girlfriend.'

I decided it would be best to be honest with her. If nothing else, it would change the subject. 'If you must know,' I began, in as benign a tone as I could, 'I found something cool. I went out walking and came across this old stone cottage. I've got no idea of the date or anything but it's just there, in the middle of these woods.' I glossed over the details.

She looked at me as if I'd gone mad, so I pulled out the metal seal from my coat pocket. 'Look, I found this. It's an old wax sealing device.'

She picked it up and tossed it from one hand to the other. 'What, so this is some kind of antique? Like, valuable and stuff?'

'Well, I guess it might be, but I'm more interested in dating it, finding out whose seal it was, you know. Just digging down into the history a bit. I'm going to have a look on the internet when I get back. Maybe go talk to Professor Makepeace about it.'

'Jesus, Daniel. You're so obsessed with all this stupid history bullshit, it's really sad.' She got up and walked out the room, feigning anger but I could sense she was still relieved by my admission that I didn't have a girlfriend. As she closed the door and dumped the seal on the table by the living room door, I slammed my fist down onto my desk. I knew I would have to tread very carefully with her in the future to avoid either hurting her or leading her on, but wasn't even sure myself how best to react here. It was all too much for me to think about, on top of everything else going on in my life.

My shift at the bar passed slowly and I found myself making stupid mistakes as a result of being so preoccupied and anxious to get back home. When I finally returned in the middle of the night, I logged straight onto the internet and began to search for information on wax sealing. There were several hobbyist websites devoted to the art of it but few that displayed old seals. I eventually found what seemed to be a fairly comprehensive collection of seal design for 17th century West Country gentry but, unsurprisingly, the seal I'd found in Wickstow was not amongst these. It was apparent even to me that the seal represented that of a tradesman and, if the tools were anything to go by, a stonemason. I tried innumerable variations on my search but came up blank each time.

It then dawned on me to try searching for the word above the cottage – 'Lambkin'. I wasn't entirely sure what I was looking for but the most frequent result seemed to link back to an old English folk ballad that bore the name 'Lambkin'. Mysteriously, no one could date the ballad itself, nor pinpoint its geographical origin. Regional variants existed all the way from Cornwall to the Scottish Highlands and the story itself seemed to grow and change with each version. Although it had clearly existed for many years prior, a 19th century book of ballads for children seemed to be the earliest printed edition and appeared to be based on one of the Scottish variations:

'LAMBKIN was as brave a builder
As eer built a stane,
And he built Lord Cassillis house,
an for payment he gat nane.

My lord said to my lady,
when he went abroad,
Tak care o fause Lambkin,
for he sleeps in the wood.'

A typically cautionary tale, the likes of which we British seem to have enjoyed scaring our children with since the dawn of time, the unexpurgated legend has it that Lambkin was a highly skilled stonemason, commissioned to build a castle for a Lord who never paid him. When the castle was complete, Lambkin demanded payment for his work and the Lord laughed in his face. Lambkin waited for many months in the nearby forests and, when the Lord went riding out to another town one day, the mason sneaked into the castle and killed his enemy's wife and young child.

Some variants of the ballad have Lambkin bathing himself in the child's blood for reasons never properly explained. It has been speculated that Lambkin may have been a leper, seeking to cure his disease by bathing in the blood of an innocent or even that it was somehow related to occult ritual. Lambkin's eventual fate is equally vague. Some versions of the ballad have him hanged. Others burnt or even drowned. A few leave things open, with Lambkin fleeing in the moonlight.

Later versions of the ballad depict Lambkin as more of an evil, otherworldly creature, rather than a disgruntled stonemason and it amused me to see that, essentially, the mentality of tabloid exaggeration was as prevalent in past times as it is now. Why let facts get in the way of a good story? Of course, due to the incredible level of variation within the different versions of the ballad, it seemed unlikely anyone would ever find the truth behind who Lambkin was or what actually happened.

That said, the more I read, the more excited I became. Everything seemed to fall into place for me and I was certain the poem was connected to the cottage in Wickstow. The seal was clearly that of a stonemason's and the letter L coupled with the name above the door could place it as being only one person's. It was situated in woodlands near a castle, so it made sense to think that the cottage was built by Lambkin, in the darkest part of the wood, as a base to hide in whilst waiting for the cheating Lord to leave the locality.

Even the local folklore that the cottage was haunted pointed in this direction. Although no one of the current generation would know exactly who or what the boogeyman was, there was certainly weight to the theory of the stories originating with the legend of Lambkin. I was suddenly ablaze with enthusiasm. It seemed as if I had potentially stumbled upon something of importance, purely by accident, and could finally make my mark on the community of historians I'd been so longing to be a real part of.

I was awake until nearly four in the morning, reading as many versions of the ballad as I could find and taking notes before eventually my eyes became too heavy to stay open and I collapsed into dreamless sleep on top of the bedcovers.

I overslept on Wednesday and it was after midday already by the time I finally roused myself. With a groan and a snarl, I lurched out of bed and made for the shower. I heard Billie scream, 'Argh! The walking dead!' in mock horror from the other room so I stuck my middle finger up in her general direction.

When I came back, she had made me a cup of coffee, which I accepted gratefully.

'So what are you up to this afternoon?' she asked.

'I was going to go back to that cottage and have a look for some more stuff. I think I might be on to something but I need a bit more proof, before I can really be sure.'

'Boring!'

'So how about you then?'

'Well, I'm looking after Melissa for Toni tonight, so I'm probably just going to chill out this afternoon, watch some 'American Idol' or something. I was thinking maybe tomorrow we could have our night in, yeah? Order pizza, just like old times? Maybe a bottle of wine?'

'Alright, sure,' I said, uncomfortably. There was a pause as I slurped my coffee, hurrying to finish it. I was eager to get going.

'You haven't asked how the job search is going,' she reminded me.

'Oh. Well?'

'Since you *ask*,' she began sarcastically, 'very well, thank you. I've got an interview on Monday with a day-care place. It's not exactly what I want to do for a career, but the pay's really good and at least I get to spend all day with kids, instead of stuck in some stuffy office somewhere.'

'Oh, good luck with that then. Let me know how it goes.' I emphasised my lack of interest, probably more than I needed to, by knocking back what was left of my coffee and discarding the cup on the table.

'God, you could sound more excited. This is a big deal for me, it's the first interview I've had in, like, months.'

'I'm sorry. I'm a bit distracted at the moment, got a few million thoughts racing through my brain all at once.'

'Whatever, it's always with the same with you. I wish you'd just show a bit of interest sometimes in something other than your stupid history.'

'I'm sorry.' She was almost making me feel guilty.

'Anyway, I'll see you tomorrow night for that pizza. You'd

better not skip out on that. If we don't start talking again, I… well… I just don't know if I can live in this flat with you any more.'

'Okay, okay, I said I'll be there. It'll be fine, okay!' I was now getting worried. If Billie were to leave the flat, I'd have no way of paying the rent single-handedly and the thought of having a total stranger move in for the remainder of the lease was terrifying. I reached out and touched her shoulder. 'It'll be cool,' I said, smiling.

'I know,' she replied and smiled back.

As she walked back into the lounge, my head began to spin with confusion. She always had a peculiar way of showing her feelings but was becoming simultaneously less rational and more annoying by the day. I tried not to think about what almost amounted to her blackmail tactics and went to pack my bag. I threw in a few cans of Pepsi, some chocolate bars, a torch, printouts of my favourite 'Lambkin' variants and, just in case I ended up screwed over by Langford's train timetables again, a sleeping bag for emergencies.

In typically British fashion, the weather was much colder than the previous day and the walk from Langford station through Lower Langford and into Wickstow was almost gruelling. Still, I had a strange and exciting sensation the further I got away from the main roads. It felt as if these were really the paths travelled by all those ancient feet in bygone times. I wondered lazily if Lambkin himself had prowled the same routes that I was now making my way down. I looked up at the trees and imagined what stories they would tell if only they could speak. I began to wish I lived out here in the country, away from all the lunacy of modern London.

By 5pm, I had found my way to the cottage again and was relieved to find that it was still there and not all just some preposterous delusion. I once more fought my way through the veil of bracken and pushed aside the creaky wooden door. The smell inside felt somehow fustier than before, damp and stale, with the cold breeze wafting the stench of mould right into my nostrils. I took the torch from my bag and proceeded to the smaller chamber.

I had no qualms about tearing up the boards surrounding the one I had already broken, or about sifting beneath them to search for further artefacts. With the torch perched precariously between my knees, I dug about in the muck for a good two hours, finding little besides bugs, earthworms and splinters. A momentary rush of excitement occurred when I discovered a rusty chisel, but there were no distinctive markings or anything tangible to link it to Lambkin. Still, if I could find out its age, I figured even this could be a vital piece of the puzzle later on. When I started to hear the fast pattering of raindrops on the stone roof, I took a break, cracked open one of the Pepsi cans and walked back to the front door, shocked to discover how torrential the downpour actually was.

The stone seemed suddenly rocked by an echo of thunder off in the distance and I saw a bolt of lightning bleed across the sky. Standing dry in the doorway, it was exhilarating to watch nature in all its glory like this. I stuck my filthy hands out into the rain and rinsed them clean, laughing as I did so, feeling a little giddy, as if I had somehow stepped back into a past time. I stopped laughing when the thought ran through my head that maybe this was exactly how Lambkin had washed the blood off his hands after he had committed murder. Maybe he had stood in this very doorway. I shuddered and went back inside.

Further search of the cottage yielded nothing else and, by about 8pm, it was pitch black outside with the storm showing no sign of easing off. The ground outside had turned into a muddy sludge and the thought of walking back through it in my trainers was not a particularly pleasant one. I sat myself down in the doorway and watched the storm for a while. The air smelt fresh and beautiful, the rain emphasising all the scents of the wood. I breathed deeply, taking it all in and enjoying the fact that, besides the storm, nothing could be heard for miles. I felt, for the first time, totally alone yet not in the least bit lonely.

I decided to stay the night in the cottage. It would be exciting and I knew that I'd never find my way out of the woods in one piece at night and with the weather as bad as it was. Besides, I'd missed the last train and another £35 for a room was more than I wanted to spend. I closed the door, unfolded my sleeping bag and wrapped myself warmly in it, using my rucksack for a pillow and trying to ignore the discomfort of the cold and dirty floor beneath me. Once I'd settled, the majestic sounds of the sky still raging outside somehow soothed me and I fell into an easy sleep.

When I awoke, it was completely dark and it took a minute or two for my eyes to adjust. Everything was silent now. The storm had clearly passed. As a result of this new silence, the sudden shuffling sound coming from the small chamber startled me all the more. I froze in fear and squinted to see if I could make out anything in the gloom. Silently, I damned myself for having left the torch in the other room.

There was definitely something moving through the archway.

It looked like a crouched human figure, slowly coming towards me. The rusty chisel I'd found was in its hand. I could hear deep, raspy breathing as it came swiftly closer. A stench of moss, lichen and rust filled my nostrils and I still found I couldn't move, even as the figure stood at the edge of my feet. It bent down and thrust its face right up close to mine.

Undoubtedly now, it was a man, but his features were covered entirely with a dark green moss. His eyes appeared milky white and without pupils. Yellow and blackened teeth protruded from his mouth and his hair, long and straggly, seemed to be made of some kind of bracken or weed. A strand of it brushed across my throat and seemed to stick there. He raised the chisel in his hands to my eye and I saw his hands and wrists were also covered completely in moss. An earthworm crawled along his fingers and threatened to fall on to my face.

'Where's'a the men of the house?' he hissed.

I was terrified into silence and had no idea how to respond. I whimpered and stammered incoherently as his other hand, muddy and moss-covered, grabbed my shirt collar.

'O still my bairn!' His voice, although barely louder than a whisper, sounded like a scream. An unearthly rage seemed to fill the cottage. 'Or I'll gie ye a peck o' goud!'

He pulled the chisel back and, before he had a chance to thrust it at me, I rolled over and knocked him sideways. As he scrambled on the floor, I realised he was completely naked although the fur-like moss was all over his body. He screamed and it sounded like a loud, high-pitched death rattle. I broke my way out of the sleeping bag and went hurtling out of the front door, smashing it off its rusty hinges as I ran.

I immediately flew head over heels, as my shoes slipped in

the slushy soil, and found myself face down in the mud. The man followed me outside and, as I stood and turned, I saw him fully in the light of the moon. Worms and beetles were crawling through the weeds that seemed to be growing out of him and I could see that dribbling out of his mouth was a flow of lumpy blood. His hands appeared to be darker than the rest of him and I realised that they too were covered with it. The awful clouded orbs in the middle of his ghastly face seemed to glow in the moonlight, as he stared straight at me.

'Pay me,' he choked, coughing up another stream of thick, almost blackened blood. 'Pay me!'

I continued running, scrambling and crawling through the mud as fast as I could, heading back to the main path through the woods, screaming for my life. There was no one around for miles. I knew that even if I were to die out here, it might take days for anyone to even find me, so I'd have no chance of rescue now. I leapt over a half-rotted stile that I remembered from the walk to the cottage and was relieved to find I was heading in the right direction. I did not look back until I reached the sign that said 'Welcome To Wickstow' and saw the dim glow of one of the village's few street lamps. I was completely out of breath and almost choking from attempts to suck more air into my lungs, but it seemed that whoever had tried to attack me in the cottage was no longer behind me.

I slowed down to a walk as I headed back toward Lower Langford and tried to make sense of what had just happened. Annoyingly, I'd left all my stuff at the cottage but nothing could've made me return at that point. The rational part of my mind told it was someone playing a practical joke, maybe one of the locals from the Bear's Head who'd overheard my conversation with the landlord's daughter. Still, part of me remained terrified by the inhuman sounds coming from the man's throat and the hideousness of his appearance. I think deep down I believed that it was Lambkin himself, in some kind of manifestation. Either that or I had completely lost my mind.

I found my way back to Langford station by about 4am, at which stage it was freezing. Too scared to go wandering, I sat myself down on the empty platform and hugged myself tight for warmth. As my teeth chattered and my skin began to crack, I realised I must have, to some extent, indeed lost my mind. It's strange how big cities can sometimes drive you to such despair that you forget yourself and just strive for escape in lieu of everything else. The claustrophobic clutter of people and buildings makes you yearn so desperately for open spaces. Yet I think the horror of running through those woods, knowing I was utterly alone and that if anything were to happen, no one would see or hear a thing… That was just too terrifying for words. The thought that whatever it was I saw could just be out there, lurking in the vast darkness, away from human eyes? I shivered, and not entirely from the cold.

By 6am, the little coffee stall on the platform had opened, so I bought a mug and held it close to me until it turned cold. It felt strange, but I was looking forward to getting back to the warmth of the flat and even seeing Billie seemed a suddenly appealing prospect. I had gone through so many emotional shifts in the last few days, I felt finally balanced again. I needed to stop being so stubborn and determined, so sure of how I wanted things to go. Instead, I needed to just let things happen naturally, to stop over-analysing events and wishing for the impossible. I was putting myself under too much pressure and situations like tonight were the end result. My psyche needed a break.

When the first train pulled into the platform at half past six, I was the only person to board it. Some sleepy commuters in suits dozed within the carriages and I sat next to the heating vent, breathing a sigh of relief to now be far away from the thing in the woods. Whether it was Lambkin or just my overactive imagination was irrelevant. Being away from it was all that counted. I slept awkwardly on the journey and was back in London before nine. The tube was crowded, as ever, but even as I was sandwiched between a sweaty delivery boy and a pushy old Indian man who kept sticking his knuckles into my back, I felt oddly safe and at home. I got some strange looks for being covered in mud, but in London, no one really bothers to ask questions. The rule is to just keep your eyes down, flash a glance and then look away again.

I picked up a box of baklava on the way in to the flat as a surprise for Billie and even yelled 'hey, how's the job search going?' when I entered the flat. She didn't respond, so I assumed she was probably still asleep. It was only when I entered the lounge that the smell hit me, vile and putrid. The walls were red all over, the carpet sticky and matted. Already, blood was congealing on the wallpaper. The television was blaring out some kind of awful reality show; the smiling, singing faces onscreen spattered with shining crimson flecks. I moved towards the TV and noticed the wash basin resting on top of it. Peering over the top, I saw the corpse of a baby inside. *Melissa*. The child Billie had been babysitting.

Melissa's tiny body was covered head to toe with large, thick needles, like some kind of human pincushion. She was floating in her own blood, which now filled the bowl. I put my hand to my mouth to try and stop the bile that was rising but it was no use. As I turned around and saw the headless remains of Billie, naked, heavily lacerated and sprawled out over the couch, I vomited all over the carpet.

My heart was beating rapidly and my head felt light. The fact that no one had found the bodies already meant that no one had seen or heard a thing, even though there were flats on either side of our own. *How could this be?*

Wiping the mist of tears out of my eyes I saw Billie's head in the corner of the room, lying in a pool of blood and shredded tendons. Dried, rust-coloured streaks adorned what was left of her neck. As I edged closer with dread, I saw that bludgeoned into the middle of her forehead was the same design as on the wax seal. Deep red and forever etched into her flesh, the snake-like L with the hammer and chisel at either side of it.

I spun round to face the table where she had left the seal. It had gone.

I sank to the floor and sat with my head in my hands, crying. With numb fingers, I called the police on my mobile, having no idea of what on Earth I could tell them to explain either what had happened or my whereabouts at the time of the murders. All I could tell them was my address, before breaking down in tears.

Lambkin's spectral voice echoed in my mind for several minutes. 'Pay me! *Pay me!*'

The lady of the house was dead. The baby had been drained dry of blood. Lambkin had his revenge. As I heard the sirens in the distance, I knew it was now time for me to pay.

The Monkey House

∴

It is a dismal Sunday afternoon. I am sitting in the study, staring out towards Jawbones Hill. There is a diabolical wind coming in from the sea. It blows dead leaves across the grounds of the house, arranging and rearranging them in meaningless patterns. Soon they will rot and be gone forever. Beneath the window, Addison's fiendish monkey is leaping amongst the briars. I flick ash from my cigarette and will it to land in the beast's eyes.

The wretched book still sits on Father's desk, daring me to persist. But I will not. *'The Descent of Man, and Selection in Relation to Sex'* by Charles Darwin. Another of Addison's anathemas. How I wish Father had never let that awful man into our home with his books and his monkey and his sinister ideas. But, of course, Father has not been the same since Mother died. I must make allowances. I must be patient with him, even if it has been several years now. Several years since London.

If we were still there, I would not be so bored and preoccupied with these thoughts of evil and death. I had to surrender so many of my pursuits when we came out here to Dartmouth, to the Bartlett family home. On a Sunday like this one four years ago, I would have been singing with my choir group. Tomorrow, I would be making for the Seven Dials with my companions from the Reformers to save the souls of the unfortunate women. The ones who doubtless still litter the cobbles, spreading their disease and malignancy to poor, weak-willed souls who know no better. Indeed there are many such souls about us. I am merely counting the hours in fact until another miserable dinner with two of them: Father and Dr. Addison.

The nuisance has been with us for several weeks now. I am unsure how long his residence will continue and have found it impossible to broach the subject without causing offence. I pray it will not be much longer but Father seems very taken with the man. He initially began corresponding with Addison whilst the doctor was working in Morocco. Father, who was always of a curious disposition in the area of hobbies, had developed a keen interest in anthropology and Africa in particular. Introduced by a mutual friend from the British Museum, Father became Addison's benefactor and, upon hearing that the latter was soon returning to Britain, offered him residence in the family home.

I can still remember his arrival. A stout little man, hopping out of the coach and waving a gnarled walking cane in greeting, pursued by that ghastly little macaque monkey he brought back from Morocco. Father finds the monkey amusing but I cannot look at its beady eyes and its snout-like nose without becoming deeply unsettled. I cannot stay calm when it's around me. I feel constantly on guard, lest it jump at me or bite me or knock me down. It possesses neither the intellect nor the morality to control its instincts and this disturbs me greatly.

I am polite with Addison but I am sure he can sense my resentment towards him. In spite of this, it is he who has loaned me the science book, imploring me to read it. I began to peruse it yesterday evening and was subsequently haunted throughout the night by horrible dreams. Even though I had closed the book after the first chapter, I remain shaken by its blasphemy even today.

Mr. Darwin begins his book by comparing the structure of man to that of a monkey, insists we are of the same general model and writes at one point that, *'it is only our natural prejudice, and that arrogance, which made our forefathers declare that they were descended from demigods.'* How can one dismiss the Creator this way? Yet he still has the nerve to accuse others of arrogance! I will have to bite my tongue at dinner. By attesting to the validity of Mr. Darwin's claims, Addison insults my ancestors. He is comparing the honourable Bartlett line to that blasted beast bouncing in the briars beneath the window. I close the curtains. I can look at the vile thing no longer.

※ ※ ※

Dinner does not pass without incident. I have taken several drops of laudanum to calm myself, following a regrettable confrontation with Addison regarding the writings of Mr. Darwin. I cannot believe that Father is allowing this despicable atheist to blaspheme beneath our own roof. Certainly he is no longer the man he was in London. Indeed, Father has not attended church on Sunday since we arrived here and I doubt that swine Addison has ever set foot in one.

I admit that after the cholera took Mother all those years ago, I found myself wondering how God could allow this to happen, how the Devil's work could triumph and claim so many innocent lives. I prayed and God sent me strength but now, with Addison's evil, I am being tested once more. I must remain true to the light of the Holy Spirit even in the darkest of times but if anything, the book's ideas have only strengthened my beliefs. I simply refuse to believe in its absurd notions. If there is no Creator, if man was not made in His image… Why, the idea is simply too horrible to contemplate.

I make for the study and toss the wretched thing in the fire, page by page, watching them fold and blacken until they resemble the rotted, dead leaves in the garden outside. Surely, if there were no God, this is all we would amount to in the end too. Ashen remains. Food for the elements. Without the promise of eternal light and life in Heaven, there would be naught to aspire to. One cannot cheat earthly death but one can live well for the promise of eternal life beyond it. Dear God, why would anyone even *want* to believe these other theories? Mr. Darwin is a sick, morbid little man. I pray for his soul.

After watching the book burn, I find I am sweating abnormally. The laudanum has made me tired but I still feel anxious. I return to my chamber and call up the manservant, requesting that he bring me brandy. While waiting, I pick up my family Bible and begin to read aloud: *'So God created man in his own image, in the image of God created he him; male and female created he them. And God blessed them and God said unto them, Be fruitful and multiply, and replenish the Earth, and subdue it; and have dominion over the fish of the sea and over the fowl of the air, and over every living thing that moveth on the Earth.'*

The manservant knocks upon the door and I am startled. For a fleeting second, his face resembles that of Addison's monkey. The small, black eyes. The squashed pink nose. I blink twice and things return to normal. I dismiss him immediately and find I cannot meet his gaze. I decant three glasses of brandy, one after the other, draining them with haste. I find my hands are shaking, as I pick up my Bible again and read: *'And Adam gave names to all cattle, and to the fowl of the air, and to every beast of the field.'*

I read until I fall into unquiet sleep, the Bible resting on my chest. My dreams are vivid and unpleasant. I dream that I am waking up, walking downstairs and finding the servants have become monkeys, all dressed up like men. They are chattering loudly, incoherently, and bouncing atop the furniture in the drawing room. I am calling out for Mother. There is a coffin in the centre of the room. The lid creaks slowly open to reveal the corpse of a monkey, dressed in Mother's clothes. The corpse begins to crumple and blacken, as if it is burning, but there is no fire. I look up and see the monkeys are laughing now, pointing at me. When I look down again, the coffin is full of dead leaves. I wake up, sweating and shrieking.

It takes me a while to regain my composure. Grabbing my bedside candle, I walk to the bathroom, light up the spirit lamp and look at myself in the glass. I have not shaved for a day or two. Hair is growing across my cheeks and chin and my whiskers have become somewhat unruly since I last visited a barber. The longer I gaze at myself, the more it dawns on me with horror how simian my face looks. *I must rid myself of this unwanted fur at once!* I reach for Father's cutthroat razor and begin to shave it away.

I have just finished removing all traces of hair from my face and scalp when I hear footsteps running down the corridor. Opening the door and waving my candle, I see the outlines of Addison's monkey scampering away towards the staircase.

Somewhat startled, I pursue the creature with intent to return it to its owner at once.

I follow it down to the kitchen and suddenly notice that it is wearing one of my father's hats.

'You little swine! Give it back!' I yell, putting the candle down and waving the razor at the beast. It begins to chatter, to jump up and down. It pulls the hat down over its face, mocking me, mocking mankind itself.

I scream, 'Vile, blasphemous creature!' and slash the awful thing with the razor. My fury is such that I slash again and again, a storm cloud of fur and blood engulfing me. When I am done, the tiny shredded body of the monkey lies on the floor. I take Father's hat from its head and catch my breath when, all of a sudden, I hear the sound of someone approaching. *'Addison!'* I think to myself with alarm, snatching up the razor and fleeing for the back door of the house. I can blame the monkey's death on one of the servants, somehow or other.

Yet its blood is all over me. Viscous and slippery, I can feel it seeping beneath my fingernails. I taste its coppery flavour on my tongue. I can feel some of it drying on my skin as I slip out into the night air. I decide to head for the coast and wash myself clean in the sea. The evening is frightfully cold but I cannot return to the house like this.

However, as I descend Jawbones Hill and the coast comes into view, I feel a strange emptiness hanging in the air. The wind has stopped now. The sky seems barren. The sea is stock-still and looks like a blanket of blackness, stretched out as far as the eye can see. The clouds appear like huge grey pillows. *Is God sleeping?* I do not feel His presence here. I feel afraid.

There is something in the water, floating towards the shore.

As I get closer to the water's edge I can make it out as a large black boat. It is moving slowly, creeping across the water like a gigantic mollusc. There are torches burning on the deck, illuminating the shadow forms of people on board.

As the boat comes closer, I begin to wade, splashing the seawater against my skin, turning it slowly crimson with the monkey's blood. When I look up, I can now clearly make out the people on the boat. They are dressed in soldier's uniforms. Red and gold coatees, bell-topped shakos. Some of them are brandishing swords.

By the time I am clean, shivering now in the cold of the night, they are close enough for me to make out their faces; their small, round heads with large black eyes, shining reddish-orange in the glow of the torches. They have bushy white eyebrows, and their faces are covered in thick grey fur. One of them turns around and shrieks to several of the others. As it spins, I see its tail swishing in the light. I am so frightened I am unable to move.

The monkey at the front moves aside to reveal two more pushing a cannon towards the front of the deck. I realise that, for the moment, God has turned His head and looked away. I know that these abominations have come for me. I know that soon I will be nothing more than dead skin and bone, then rotted debris to be blown across the beach with the pebbles and the seaweed.

'Yea, though I walk through the valley of the shadow of death, I will fear no evil,' I begin to mutter, splashing through the sea, waving my razor in vain at the monkeys on the boat. My skin is numb from the icy ocean spray and saltwater is seeping into open cuts I had previously not noticed were there. *'Thou art*

with me, thy rod and thy staff they comfort me,' I intone, but the words have become meaningless.

Nostalgia Ain't What It Used To Be

⁖

'Birth is not a beginning; death is not an end. There is existence without limitation; there is continuity without a starting point. Existence without limitation is Space. Continuity without a starting point is Time. There is birth, there is death, there is issuing forth, there is entering in.'
CHUANG TZU

'Katie McDonald was never really here. Katie McDonald is everywhere and nowhere.'

The words echoed in Katie's head, entwining with the persistent beep of the alarm clock. She couldn't place the context nor recognise the wavering, faintly accented voice that whispered them. If she could've held onto them a little longer she may have remembered that she had heard them before. Many times. They dissolved as she blinked her eyes and cleared the hazy red mist that lingered from the dream.

It was already 6:30am. She raised a tired arm to shut off the clock. Another Monday morning had rolled around and this one felt worse than usual thanks to the stale taste and the dull ache left behind by last night's bottle of Tesco Chardonnay. She dragged herself out of bed and into the living room. The empty bottle and wine glass she'd left on the coffee table mocked her.

It wasn't Katie's style to drink on a work night. This rare

indulgence was because that stupid, cheap brand of wine – not even pleasant to taste – reminded her of Michael. She'd thrown a couple of bottles into her shopping basket in a weird fit of nostalgia and had sat by herself on the sofa, sipping at one and remembering times not long past.

Michael had not been a wine expert nor a big spender and this particular Chardonnay had been the one he'd always brought round to the flat when he and Katie had arranged for a romantic night in. She assumed that the first time he got it was because it was the cheapest one he could find and then he'd just stuck with it since Katie never complained. He probably thought it was her favourite, although truth be told, she much preferred a nice Malbec.

As Katie prepared her morning coffee, she winced at the memory that hit her. Towards the end of the bottle, she'd actually switched the TV over to the Discovery Channel and watched a wildlife documentary. That's how bad it had got. She flushed with shame.

Animal husbandry had been Michael's hobby. Even on their romantic nights in, he would invariably change the subject of conversation to farming trivia and they'd end up curled up on the sofa, Chardonnay in hand, watching a documentary about sheep farming in the Falklands or some such.

Initially, Katie had found this rather endearing; she liked a man with interests and some of his more unusual anecdotes would make her laugh.

'I've been thinking about something, Fluffykins,' he'd exclaim. She was never entirely sure about 'Fluffykins' as a pet name but let it slide as he seemed to delight in it. 'Lesbian ewes must live in such sufferance.'

'Lesbian ewes?' she'd reply, raising an eyebrow in anticipation of the punchline.

'Well, you see, during estrus when a ewe is in heat, she stands perfectly still waiting to be mounted. This can last for anything up to 30 hours before the ram, who is fertile all year and has no such restrictions regarding his mobility, takes her. I was thinking; what if two ewes were attracted to one another? They'd see each other, immediately go into heat but have to just stand there, perfectly motionless, unable to consummate their passions! It must be Hell!'

Then both Katie and Michael would laugh uproariously.

However, four years of these obscure observations and little else made Katie feel like one of those poor ewes herself. Michael's lovemaking, when it happened at all, was brief and uninspired. If he could've shown as much excitement towards Katie as he did at the news of a six-part documentary they could watch together (usually in one sitting, thanks to the ghastly SkyPlus box he installed for her), perhaps they'd still be together.

But enough was enough. She'd taken him aside one night last month, they'd talked frankly and the evening had ended with polite handshakes and an assurance they'd remain friends. They hadn't spoken since.

At first being free of him had been a relief. The discomfort that crawled beneath her skin and pricked at her with pointed questions about their future had gone away and the world seemed once again open with opportunity. She'd vowed to never watch another second of the Discovery Channel and instead spent her evenings enjoying the latest blockbusters on Sky Movies. The freedom felt good. She could now attend work functions without the fear that he would embarrass her by waxing lyrical to her bosses about shortening the tails of newborn lambs. She didn't have to answer to anyone, take responsibility for anyone or justify why she was watching 'Along Came Polly' for the fourth time that week. She just was.

So what had prompted the spontaneous Chardonnay? The simple answer was that she missed having Michael around. It was nice not to listen to him waffle on but there was a hole where he once was. She no longer had anyone to sound off at about the stresses of the working day. Just having someone to touch affectionately or to cuddle with in bed was a comfort she found herself missing. Michael was boring but he was a safe bet. He would've been there for as long as she'd've had him around and, in her darker moments, she chastised herself for daring to want better.

Katie was 36 years old. She disliked her mundane job in Order Administration and, whilst she'd always been a 'live for the weekend' type, she was fast realising that the weekend had little better to offer. She had lost touch with most of her old friends and socialised only with the girls from work, most of whom she suspected mocked her (and, specifically, her age) behind her back. The last week had been and gone in a blur of data entry, microwaveable low-fat lasagnes and broken sleep. She dreaded that this week would be the same.

She pulled open the curtains to let in the first rays of July morning sunshine, made a cup of tea, showered, and used the toilet, letting the grim aftermath of the Chardonnay binge wash itself down the drain. As she dried her hair, dressed for work and put on her make-up, she softly sang 'A Good Heart' by Feargal Sharkey; a song she'd loved in the 80s that held particular resonance for her now.

'Aye, you're right, Feargal,' she mused as she picked up her house keys. 'A good heart these days *is* hard to find.'

Refreshed and rattling with the ibuprofen she'd exceeded the stated dose of, Katie walked down Highgate Road from her flat, heading towards Kentish Town underground station. It was going to be another hot, clammy day in London. The sunshine now started to hurt her eyes a little and she wished she had a pair of sunglasses.

As she approached the station, she passed the grubby little market stall selling miscellaneous junk. It was manned by an elderly Chinese man. She'd seen him there most mornings but had never actually looked at what he had to sell, assuming it would all be useless. However, that morning, she spotted a rack of sunglasses for £1 each and decided this would be a wise investment. As she picked up the most discreetly coloured pair she could find, she scanned the rest of the man's stall and was impressed by the weird diversity of merchandise. He sold everything from batteries to bath salts to boxes of old newspapers that, according to their labels, dated at least as far back as the 1940s.

What caught Katie's eye, however, was a selection of CDs laid out in the middle of the stall, also priced at £1 a piece. In the four years she'd been dating Michael, her love of music had dwindled. He never shared much interest in it and she scarcely found the time to listen anyway, as she juggled work and a relationship. Recently, she'd picked up the latest CDs by Coldplay and Snow Patrol, two British guitar bands that her workmates had recommended. The Coldplay one had sent her to sleep when she'd tried listening to it. She didn't dislike it but it just didn't spark the same passion for her that music used to back in the 80s. Back then, it had been the vibrant soundtrack to her life and emotions. It had painted with melodies things she couldn't express in words.

That was it, she decided. The missing link. She needed to listen to more music. That would perk her up. Scanning the CDs on the old Chinese man's stall, she picked out a compilation of various artists called 'From Yazoo To Yazz - The Greatest Hits of the 80s!' that was definitely worth a quid. She knew at least 90% of the songs on it by heart and yet no longer had copies of them.

'Why not?' she said, plucking a £2 coin from her bag and buying both the CD and the sunglasses.

'Why not?' chuckled the old Chinese man, like an echo. 'Why not? You have good day, why not?'

'Why not indeed?' replied Katie with a smile.

The day at work was typically mundane and she spent much of it humming songs from the 80s to herself, counting the hours until she could go home, crack open a bottle of cold Chardonnay and have a little boogie round the living room. Just a couple of glasses to take the edge off tonight, mind. Not the whole thing.

The Purchasing department of HBG Telecoms was well air-conditioned. This was about the only positive thing Katie could say about her job there. It was a thankless, monotonous data entry job and she shared a partitioned four-way desk with Fiona, Mandy and Asha, the other Order Admin girls. Technically, her title was 'Team Leader' but she suspected that middle management had given her this as an act of mercy, to soften the embarrassment of her being at least 10 years older than any of the other girls. Katie did very little in the way of leadership. It more or less meant picking up the slack when the other girls were off sick with hangovers. The ogre-like Julie Ford, a short Irish redhead who adhered to all three stereotypes, managed them all with an iron fist. An iron fist that perpetually clutched a red biro used for highlighting mistakes in data entry. These corrections often came accompanied with a cruel personal insult.

Katie was midway through humming 'She Drives Me Crazy' by Fine Young Cannibals when Julie left her glass booth at the end of the open plan office. This always meant bad news. Katie heard a chorus line of mouse clicks as a dozen or so internet browser windows were closed down in fright.

'Right! Listen up, team!' barked Julie in her loud, smoke-ravaged Dublin drawl. 'Overtime tonight! There's no way we're gonna fill those wee orders for Merrill, 'less we get crackin' on buyin' all of them widgets.' Katie hated how Julie would collectively refer to all telecoms hardware as widgets. It made a demeaning task feel even more demeaning and pointless.

All four girls looked at one another over the top of their partitions and Mandy rolled her eyes at Katie.

'Good!' piped Julie, fishing a cigarette packet from her pocket. 'Glad you're all okay with that, so I am. Dave'll be emailin' you the first of the orders soon.' With that, she made for the corridor, leaving the girls to sigh and curse her under their breath.

'I don't believe this,' snarled Asha. 'I've got a date tonight.'

'Well,' began Katie, meekly. 'You don't *have* to do the

overtime. It's not like it's paid or anything.'

'Of course I have to do it. I wanna keep my job, don't I?' replied Asha, already tapping out a frantic text message on her mobile. 'You know what the bitch is like.'

Katie sighed and her mind began wandering to the first job she had, working for a small family-owned construction company just outside Edinburgh. They'd always paid fairly for overtime. Volunteered extra contributions to the company's welfare were valued, as opposed to just expected. The relationship with her boss then was far more give and take. Maybe it was just London, but nowadays it seemed that everyone just existed for the sake of their jobs and for getting ahead, even if it meant becoming a doormat for the company and losing out on having any kind of a life outside it.

Asha was the youngest of the four Order Admin girls and was particularly typical of this attitude. Katie would never have entertained the idea of cancelling a previously arranged date in favour of unpaid overtime sprung on her at the last minute, but Asha accepted it like second nature; just a few short barks of discontent before rolling over. Then again, the odds of Katie having a previously arranged date at all were slimmer than her youthful colleague's annoyingly impeccable waistline. She too fell into the trap of frequent unpaid overtime if only for lack of having anything better to do.

At least tonight she could listen to her new CD when she got home. Humming Erasure's 'A Little Respect' to herself, Katie wondered how things got so strange and at exactly which point in time the world stopped making sense to her.

In the end, the overtime wasn't too bad. The girls all knuckled down and Katie finally got back home to Kentish Town around 8pm. It was still light out and the summer heat lingered in the air. She deflated on the sofa and lay there for a little while, limp and sleepy, before heading over to the kitchen and making dinner. Without Michael around to compliment her on her cooking, Katie became lazy. It wasn't easy to buy ingredients in small quantities and her freezer wasn't large enough to store leftovers so, rather than go to all the trouble, she currently existed on a diet of Findus Lean Cuisine ready-meals.

Monday night's low-fat lasagne was as bland as Friday's had been. Katie was glad to get it over with and pop the bottle of £3.19 Chardonnay which, for a change, actually tasted quite pleasing after such a hard, hot day at work.

After downing most of her first glass in one enthusiastic gulp, Katie switched on the CD player and slipped the 80s compilation into its waiting jaws. For the next 70 minutes, she danced around the living room in a reverie, listening to tunes she hadn't heard for over a decade, awash with wonderful memories. It was Duran Duran's 'Rio' that triggered the most. It reminded her just how much she'd worshipped at this band's altar throughout most of her senior school years.

'Her name is Rio and she dances on the sand…'

Like many of her friends' bedrooms, Katie's had been plastered with posters of Duran Duran's singer, Simon Le Bon. You could barely see an inch of dull beige paintwork behind all the black leather, crushed velvet and silk shirts. As he now roared the words to 'Rio' through her speakers, memories of that room came flooding back to her.

'Just like that river drifting through the dusty land…'

Katie had a happy childhood. She was born an only child in Stockbridge, a suburb of Edinburgh, and had been spoilt rotten by her mum and dad. She would receive home-made dollhouses from her dad every birthday and be encouraged to make her own accessories for them throughout the year. As a girl, Katie would dream about being a doll herself, living inside one of those dream houses. She would be surrounded by beautiful architecture, a handsome husband, two wee babies in ornamental cots and, of course, a doll's wardrobe full of elaborate, elegant outfits especially designed for her.

'And when she shines she really shows you all she can…'

As she'd moved into her teenage years she stopped playing with the toys, but the fantasies continued, as wide-eyed and as innocent as they'd been back then. She used to wish Simon Le Bon would be her doll husband, living with her in the dream home, and their first baby would be called, of course, Rio. Their second, perhaps Barbarella?

'Oh Rio, Rio, dance across the Rio Grande…'

Katie let out a wistful sigh and wondered what Simon Le Bon was doing right now. Maybe she could find a way of getting in touch with him. She wondered if he had his phoneline with HBG Telecoms. Maybe she could use that as an in-road. Slightly overcome by her nostalgia and the third large glass of Chardonnay, she felt strangely teenaged again and began giggling for no apparent reason. It was a nice feeling of amusement and arousal combined. With her head and heart buried in the past, Katie felt optimistic about the future for the first time in months.

'Rio' finished on that gloriously dramatic synth flourish, and the next track on the album kicked in. It was 'The Only

Way is Up', a one-hit-wonder from 1989 by Yazz and the Plastic Population. This one had been released around the time Katie was starting her first job and, for the second time that day, her thoughts drifted fondly back to that nice little construction company just outside of Edinburgh. She and the other data entry girls, who were – unlike nowadays – all around the same age as Katie, would go clubbing every Friday in the city and this song, silly as it was, brought those carefree memories back to the forefront.

Clubbing now was too heady for Katie, especially in London. She found it was less about enjoying the music and more just about showing off designer label clothes. Plus, there were all the drugs. Katie believed that girls didn't need drugs to have fun in the 80s. It was a far more innocent time. But then, listening to what passed for music these days, Katie could almost understand the impetus to enhance it with chemicals. To her ears, it was just a booming juggernaut of endless techno beats, precious few lyrics and even fewer melodies. Everything had a rap in it. But Yazz. That was real music. With a tune.

'The only way is UP!' shouted Katie in time to the CD, whipping her hair like she'd stepped out of a shampoo advert. 'Woo! Baby! For you and me!'

After the fourth glass of Chardonnay had been happily glugged down, the bottle was empty and the CD was in its second full rotation. At this stage, a mad idea struck Katie and she went rifling through her drawers to find an old Global Hypercolour T-shirt she'd bought in 1989.

It was far too tight in places, but just about fit her after a struggle and she was amused to note that it still changed colour when she pressed her hand to it. She giggled to herself, remembering how fashionable these colour-changing tops were at the tail end of the 80s. Skipping the CD forward to the Yazz track from earlier, she danced in her Hypercolour shirt and sang along for another half hour until the wine went to her head and she passed out on the sofa, hi-fi still blaring.

'*The only way is up (woo!) baby... for you and me...*'

※ ※ ※

The next morning, Katie woke up feeling very rough indeed from a combination of the hangover (worsened by the cumulative effect of two-night drinking), the hard sofa, the unexpected exercise of so much dancing and from another strange dream that faded from her grasp before she could recall the details.

Nevertheless, she braved the curtains, let in the sunshine, showered, downed ibuprofen with cranberry juice and staggered to the tube station, £1 sunglasses firmly affixed to her eyes. The old Chinese man with the market stall bowed in greeting and she smiled weakly back at him. The smile broadened however when she noticed a new addition to the bargain CD selection - 'The Best of Duran Duran'.

She bought it straight away and passed much of the day at work singing 'Rio' and 'Hungry Like The Wolf' at her desk, much to the chagrin of Fiona and Mandy who kept rolling their eyes at one another and looking at Katie as if she were mad. Even the demonic Julie Ford couldn't break Katie's mood today though. It had perked right up as soon as the hangover had worn off.

For lunch, she passed the drinks machine and bought a can

of full-sugar Coca-Cola 'Classic' as it was now called. It was the first time she'd had it since the 80s – the decade in which the artificial sweetener came to rule the lives of the fat-phobic public – and the sticky sensation on her teeth, coupled with a low-level sugar buzz, made her grin. Memories of childhood barbecues passed through her mind; her Dad serving glasses of Coke with ice cubes in them. Diet Coke hadn't even existed back then.

As she returned to her desk, smiling and licking the cola residue from her teeth, Mandy looked at the red can and exclaimed, 'Ew! You're drinking full fat! That's gross!'

Katie just giggled, rolled her eyes and sat down to a relatively painless afternoon's data entry, soundtracked by the melodies of Simon Le Bon's voice echoing in her mind.

'Her name is Rio and she dances on the sand…'

She skipped Tuesday's designated ready meal in favour of a huge Victoria sponge cake she had picked up (along with another two bottles of £3.19 Chardonnay) from Tesco on her way home. Her mother used to cook a delicious Victoria sponge and, whilst the homogenised Tesco Bakery didn't quite make it the same, it satiated her craving for more sugar and nostalgia. The cake reminded her of birthdays, which were always a pleasure back then instead of the dreary, dimly tragic non-birthdays she'd had post-30, tarnished by work and self-analysis.

She wolfed down the cake, cracked open the Chardonnay and, with curtains wide to let in the last of the day's sunshine, slipped her new Duran Duran CD into the hi-fi. 'To absent friends!' she toasted, thinking of Simon Le Bon and cranking up the volume.

After the first couple of songs, Katie slipped into her Global Hypercolour shirt and danced around the living room in just that and her underwear, wine glass in one hand, invisible microphone in the other. She sang along to 'The Reflex' and 'Planet Earth' as if every last line meant the world to her. Even a lyric like *'Every little thing the reflex does leaves you answered with a question mark'* which, if she was honest, she didn't understand in the slightest. But the music still sounded great. Time hadn't aged it.

The wine seemed to be going down faster than ever and she drank heartily between songs to keep her throat from getting hoarse through singing. After 'Girls on Film' had faded out, the familiar drum loop of the next track kicked in and Katie squealed with joy. She'd completely forgotten about this song and yet it had always been one of her favourites back in the day.

Flinging half a glass of Chardonnay over her shoulder and dropping to her knees, she closed her eyes, raised both arms skywards and sang with near-religious gusto – *'Please, please tell me now! Is there something I should know?'*

She star-jumped up from the ground, as the other instruments kicked in. She whirled around the room in rapture, turning her pastel green Hypercolour shirt pink from the heat of her exertions. Then suddenly, like gunshots, a loud and fast knocking at the front door broke the spell. Shaking her head and immediately turning down the hi-fi, Katie shouted 'Er... COMING!' and hurriedly pulled her skirt back on.

When she opened the door, a stocky middle-aged man stood there, dressed in a dirty white vest and brown corduroy trousers.

'What's going on, love?' he exclaimed in a harsh North London accent. 'I can't 'ear me Eastenders downstairs! Missus is goin' up the wall, sayin' to me what the bleedin' 'ell's goin' on 'ere and I says to her I don't know what the bleedin' 'ell's goin' on 'ere 'cos all I can 'ear is this 'ere.' He waved his hands in the direction of Katie's flat. 'So what's goin' on? You 'avin a party or somethin'? Bit much on a bleedin' Tuesday, don't you think? All bleedin' night last night too.'

Katie assumed the man must be her downstairs neighbour but they'd never met and she was startled by his sudden appearance, numbed by the embarrassment that a complete stranger had been listening to her singing her heart out. She began to stammer an explanation but it faltered. She realised she couldn't justify what a woman in her late-30s was doing dancing around her living room, half-drunk, half-naked, wearing a garishly coloured t-shirt several sizes too small for her and screaming Duran Duran at the top of her lungs.

'Uh, I'm sorry,' muttered Katie. 'It's, um, I'm sorry. I've been uh, drinking.'

'Bleedin' 'ell, love, it's half past eight in the evenin', get yourself a bleedin' coffee and sober up and, for gawd's sakes, turn that rubbish down. I 'eard enough of that floppy-'aired crap in the bleedin' 80s, din't I!'

'I'm really sorry,' said Katie, feeling her voice start to wobble.

'Can't hear me Eastenders,' the man repeated, shaking his head and already starting to walk away. 'Missus don't know what's goin' on, turns out the girl's got a bleedin' drink problem, don't it? Oh my life…' He trailed off and disappeared down the corridor with neither acknowledgement nor acceptance of Katie's apology.

As Katie sadly closed the door, she retreated to the sofa, collapsed face down on it and began crying at the absurdity of her situation. The intrusion into her reverie by this loud and sweaty downstairs neighbour had brought her crashing back down to (Planet) Earth. The party was over and now, fuelled by wine and humiliation, came the self-pity.

Katie wept and bitterly contemplated how different her life would be had it worked out how she'd planned it. She could play her music as loud as she wanted to and no one would ever hear it in her detached country house. She'd be making an elaborate seafood dinner right now for her husband, who'd be home soon from a long day at the recording studio and they'd eat it together without any cheap Tesco Chardonnay. No, it'd be only the finest Malbec. Maybe even Champagne on Fridays.

How did her life go so wrong? She had fallen so far from what she'd wanted to be on those gorgeous sunny afternoons in her parents' garden, all full-sugar Coke and sneaking upstairs to listen to her Duran Duran singles ('The Wild Boys' on 7" vinyl! Heaven!). How many times must she have had to make the wrong decision to end up so hopeless? Was it moving to London (the place she had been told 'everything' was at)? Was it just her lack of corporate ambition? Was she too 'nice'? Too unwilling to be ruthless or even, most of the time, assertive? Or just too stupid? Perhaps she was being arrogant to expect anything more than this? Was this 'it'? Or was it just that she'd spent her whole life existing inside fantasy worlds created from a past that's long gone or a future that didn't exist, rather than living in the present?

She had no answers to any of these questions. She just closed her eyes, still leaking tears, and drifted off into the arms of sleep, as Simon Le Bon sang 'Save a Prayer' gently through the stereo speakers.

'All alone ain't much fun so you're looking for the thrill and you know just what it takes and where to go... Don't say a prayer for me now... Save it for the morning after...'

❖ ❖ ❖

The morning after was a miserable affair.

The week's worth of English summer seemed to be over. The sun had gone away somewhere nicer and left its miserable cousin the rain looking after the country. As Katie opened the curtains and tried to shake once more from her head the faint recollections of a dream that was so red and so scary, she sighed at the sight of an almost sideways downpour that battered at her windowpane.

The usual morning ritual complete, Katie armed herself with an umbrella and headed up to the tube station. Owing presumably to the bad weather, the old Chinese man and his stall were not there this morning, but in the place where he normally stood, Katie noticed a small, laminated paper sign that was stuck to the wall with duct tape.

'Tired? Miserable? Longing for something better? Call Jeng Xiang – Chinese mystic – Much good fortune'

There was a phone number at the bottom with a local area code. She assumed Jeng Xiang was probably the same old Chinese man that ran the junk stall and was instantly cynical about any mystical powers he might possess but something about the ad made her want to ring the number. It played to her current weaknesses. Yes, she was tired. Yes, she was miserable and, by golly, she was looking for something better. It was a daft, desperate act perhaps but the thought of facing another day's cycle of data entry, ready meals and the ninety-millionth Sky Movies showing of 'Harry Potter and the Low-Fat Lasagne' or whatever it was called seemed too pathetic to contemplate.

Katie pulled out her mobile and punched in the number, ducking for cover in the entrance of the tube station.

'Hello?' said a wavering, faintly accented voice on the other end.

'Um, hi, is that Jeng Zy…ang?' asked Katie, struggling with the pronunciation.

'Yes yes, this Jeng Xiang, how may I be of service today?'

'Um, well, I saw your poster. I'm, er, longing for something better…'

'Ah! Yes, of course! Something better, something better. Please come. I will make appointment. When you make it here? To shop? Right now?'

'Oh, no, I'm not sure I can make…' Katie paused. What was stopping her from just going? She could tell Julie she had a doctor's appointment, be done with Jeng Xiang in probably less than an hour and be at work long before lunchtime with no one any the wiser. She felt impatient. She wanted to see him as soon as possible, if only to add a bit of colour and variety to the week. Any of the promised 'much good fortune' would just be a bonus.

'Actually. Yes,' she said, assertively. 'Right now would be fine. Where are you?'

'Kentish Town. On Griffin Road. Number 88. You see my sign. Yes. Doctor shop of many herbs and cures.'

'Oh, I'm not far from there,' said Katie. 'I should be able to get there in 10 minutes or so.'

'10 minutes is good. 10 minutes. And who shall I expect to see?'

'Katie McDonald.'

'Ah yes, Katie McDonald,' he repeated and Katie felt the strangest sense of déjà vu.

※ ※ ※

Katie stood outside 88 Griffin Road in the pouring rain, feeling deeply ridiculous. It was a run-down looking shop front. Scrappy paper posters hung in the window, offering sexual stimulant herbs in varying degrees of broken English. With a sigh of resignation, she pushed open the glass door and entered. The air was thick with fragrant smoke. The old Chinese man stood at a counter, behind a trio of burning joss sticks. He was surrounded by strange, smoky jars with unclear contents. It reminded Katie a little of an old-fashioned sweet shop gone very wrong.

'Ah! Katie McDonald,' he said, smiling and opening his arms.

'Yes, that's right. You must be Jeng Xiang.'

He nodded.

'You run a stall by the station as well as this, right?'

He nodded again. 'Yes, I have stall. Everything you want on stall. Why not?' He smiled again. 'Come, come.'

He pushed back some hanging beads and walked through a doorway behind them. Katie followed him into the other room. The walls in there were adorned with scrolls. Each bore pictures, with Chinese lettering underneath. A young boy in the park; a four leaf clover; other, more cryptic, images; all painted in deep, dark brush-strokes. A paper lantern dangling from the ceiling provided the only illumination. There was little furniture in the room; just a bookcase, full of hardcovers with indecipherable Chinese titles, and a large leather sofa.

'Please, take seat here,' said Jeng Xiang, gesturing towards it.

Katie sat down and asked, 'Err, what exactly do you do here?'

'Ah! Much good fortune. I make you happy like you were when you little girl.'

'Alrighty then,' she said. This was getting a bit strange. She began to worry that he might be some sort of pervert. She remembered a small can of Sure deodorant in her handbag and subtly fished around for it, as Jeng Xiang went into another room. She found it and gripped it tightly within her fist. She could, at least, use the can like Mace if the need arose.

The old man returned about a minute later with a small wooden chair, which he placed by the sofa. He sat down on it.

'I want you lie down and close eyes,' he said and smiled again.

Pulse racing, Katie lay back on the couch and tried to keep him talking. 'Is this some kind of hypnotism?' she asked.

'Some kind of hypnotism, yes. Some kind,' replied Jeng Xiang.

Katie reluctantly closed her eyes and tightened her grip on the Sure can.

Jeng Xiang's voice lowered to a whisper. 'Katie McDonald,' he began. 'I sense you not happy. I sense you longing for something you not have and you maybe have before?'

Katie nodded, but didn't say anything, partially out of fear and partially because she was beginning to feel a little faint.

'I sense you want to go back to time earlier in life.'

Katie nodded once more, the fear now being eclipsed entirely by a dizzy sort of sleepiness. Her grip on the deodorant loosened and the can dropped to the floor. She heard it roll away.

'I sense you like to be where you were most happy. I want you tell me this time and we go there. You go there. Tell me your place where you most happy.'

Katie spoke dreamily and slowly. 'I don't know,' she mumbled.

'Tell me your place,' reiterated Jeng Xiang.

'I don't know, I don't know.'

Through the haze, Katie struggled to think of when she'd been most happy and, in the altered state of consciousness she now found herself, began floating vividly through her memories. They were different to the ones she'd been enjoying for the past few days; more real somehow.

Her happiness. Where was it?

Her time with Michael had been peppered with pleasant times but overall, as much as she occasionally missed it, their relationship had been more of a chore than a joy.

Her memories of working at the construction firm in Edinburgh were alright but tainted with days wasted on boring data entry, not all that far removed from the present. Those early years of adulthood at the clubs, filled with drunken laughter and dancing as they may have been on a good night, all seemed to end with her being alone when the music stopped. It's funny how she'd forgotten the many times that she'd come home from the club crying and wondering what was wrong with her.

Farther back, the memories of her high school years in the room of the Duran Duran wallpaper were equally mixed. She'd been a lonely, frumpy teenager and whilst her friends had been pairing off with boys, she'd spent hours listening to 'Save a Prayer' on repeat and dreaming away, gloomily not wistfully, of Simon Le Bon. The dream had seemed hopeless even then. If Jocky MacKenzie from the sixth form wouldn't go out with her, what chance did she have with Simon Le Bon?

Those childhood barbecues and birthdays had their fair share of unhappiness too, like the time her boisterous cousins were invited to her party and they wrecked one of her dollhouses. Or the times her father would overdo it on the Scotch and threaten to walk out on them if he couldn't have his way over some meaningless argument or other. No wonder Katie had spent so much time lost in the fantasies of her dolls. Bits of wood and plastic couldn't argue, hurt or even speak.

'I don't know,' said Katie again. Tears poured from her closed eyes and she felt them run down her cheeks and onto the leather couch. 'I really don't know where I was ever happy.'

'I know,' said Jeng Xiang. 'I know your place, Katie McDonald.'

'K..Katie McDonald…' she sobbed.

'Katie McDonald was never really here. Katie McDonald is everywhere and nowhere.' Jeng Xiang hissed and everything stopped.

※ ※ ※

Katie found herself somewhere very red.

'Katie McDonald was never really here. Katie McDonald is everywhere and nowhere.'

The words echoed in Katie's head, entwining with a persistent beating. It was a heartbeat. Her own, perhaps? Words and thoughts fell from her mind. She could feel herself unlearning everything she'd known. At first she fought against it, fearing that she was having some kind of brain haemorrhage but, as the concept of what brain haemorrhages even were withdrew from her memory banks, she began to calmly accept it. Eventually, her thoughts were blank. She stuck her thumb in her mouth and listened to the gentle sound of her heartbeat.

'Katie McDonald was never really here.'

If she listened carefully, beyond the soft sound of the liquid waves lapping around her ears, she could hear another heartbeat somewhere beyond the red. She was floating somewhere beautiful, somewhere safe. This other heartbeat was a comforting sound and, before long, she'd instinctively brought her own down to match it. The two hearts beat as one and she knew that this other person, out there beyond the red, would keep her safe. She felt nothing, knew nothing beyond comfort and hope.

The future would be whatever it would be.

'…never really here…'

It was Thursday morning. Jeng Xiang straightened up his stall in the newly reborn July sunshine and smiled at the commuters heading into Kentish Town tube station. He tidied up the CD racks, carefully putting 'The Best of Duran Duran' and the 80s compilation back into their rightful place. He sifted through the boxes of papers, rearranging one or two of them that had fallen out of chronological order.

He had today's paper by his side and leafed through it after the rush hour had finished and he'd made most of his sales for the day. He particularly enjoyed the births and deaths section, as ever, and was pleased to note, beneath it, a small advert for Duran Duran's upcoming gig at Wembley Arena and their new album. Everything felt right today.

Jeng Xiang smiled and sang a little song to himself. *'Every little thing the reflex does leaves you answered with a question mark...'* Maybe the words did mean more than the likes of Katie McDonald would ever understand. Maybe she would never find out. But Jeng Xiang knew. He was in charge of finding treasure in the dark.

Gaijin

⋯

When the coach drove back out into the darkness, I was alone. The station had shut down by this time. It was strange to think of it even existing prior to my arrival. Like a fridge that's dark inside until you open the door and trigger the lights, it felt as though the building had just materialised from nothing when it sensed the coach's arrival.

Of course, such thoughts were silly but I'd seen little outside to suggest there was much nearby in the way of civilisation. A long, flat road had led here and the strip lights that currently lit the grey concrete walls and the asphalt concourse were the only source of illumination for at least a couple of miles.

It wasn't the first coach station I'd seen like this recently but these odd little buildings outside of the big cities were often busy during the day. They teemed with people going back and forth whose appearance and speech helped you distinguish where you were. By night, however, they all looked the same. Only the signage gave any indication as to where you could be. That said, nowadays, even most of that was written in several different languages. I could've been anywhere but, more accurately, I was nowhere.

As usual, no one was waiting for me. I was only here to transfer on to my next coach. The woman at the Tourist Information Centre in the city had sold me my journey tickets and, upon seeing my rucksack, tried to give me pointers on travelling. I was unfamiliar with the country and had tried to scrawl down everything she told me on a piece of paper but she talked too fast for me to keep up. My notes were nonsense.

To pass the time and keep warm, I walked a circuit around the hangar-like building. There were a couple of closed doorways leading into toilets and private offices but otherwise, this was it. Several rows of red moulded plastic chairs sat back to back from one another by the wall. The ticket booths were locked and empty. The only sounds were a gentle wind flowing in through the huge coach entrance and the electric hum of a drinks machine.

A grey clock hung on a wall and presumably ticked but it was too far away for me to hear it. There was no second hand on the face, which made me feel as if time was standing still when I looked at it. If I turned away and looked back a little later, the time had always moved forward but when I stared at it, willing it to move before my eyes, the clock defiantly refused.

When I tired of the clock game, I peered through the slats of a closed sandwich shop and saw one or two filled bread rolls had been left in a display case, waiting to be sold. Yesterday's bread, freshly made tomorrow. Today, for them, was an irrelevance and might as well not exist.

A movement caught my eye and I saw a dead leaf bounce across the concourse in the breeze. It looked so out of place amongst the concrete that I picked it up and slipped it in my pocket. A souvenir to maybe show to someone, somewhere at some point. Proof that I'd been here, on the outskirts of this foreign city, if only for a little while.

My rucksack began to ache on my shoulders so I placed

it on the floor and sat down on one of the red plastic chairs. A primitive electronic sign hung from the ceiling in front of me and listed the route numbers of the coaches due for arrival. At this time of the morning, they were few and far between.

I sank back into the seat just as the door to the toilet opened and a girl walked out. I was surprised to see someone else and wondered how long she'd been in there. She came and sat in the same row of chairs as me but not in the seat directly adjacent. I pretended to study the arrivals sign intently. It was one of those moments where I understood why people smoked: to make it look like they were active. Few things are as embarrassing as a stranger watching you do nothing. Relaxation is such a private pursuit that it feels shameful to share it.

'Have you got a cigarette?' she asked, as if reading my mind. I couldn't quite place her accent but was relieved that we both spoke the same language.

'I'm sorry, no,' I replied.

She nodded and we sat in silence once more.

'Shame,' she murmured after a minute or so. 'I feel like I could stay in this place forever if I just had enough cigarettes. It's so quiet.'

I smiled, apologetically. 'Sorry.'

We lapsed into silence again. I stole a quick glance at her, just to check she wasn't staring at me expectantly. She was quite pretty although she had dirty hair, tied tightly behind her head, and her eyes were red and puffy as if she'd been up all night. Perhaps she had. I glanced again at the grey clock, which had leapt forward once more when I wasn't looking, although the game wasn't as much fun any more. The girl's presence had ruined it by confirming that time was in fact moving as normal.

'Hey, I think I'm on the E32 route,' I said, pulling out the scrap of paper onto which I'd scrawled the details. 'I'm not really sure though. I'm supposed to be changing here. I don't suppose you know if this is the right coach? I'm heading to…'

She cut me off. 'I'm really sorry. I'm not from around here and I don't really know it too well. I'm just trying to get home. I'm getting the E19. Sorry.'

'Oh, that's okay,' I said, chuckling nervously. 'I'm sure everything will work out alright in the end.'

'Thank you,' she said dreamily, then turned her head away from me as if suddenly realising that we were talking at cross-purposes.

I felt like apologising but didn't want to offend her so we lapsed back into silence, albeit a slightly more awkward one than before. I got up to buy a can of something from the drinks machine, even though I wasn't thirsty.

Thankfully, as I made my way back to the red seats, a loud rumble and two bright lights heralded the arrival of the E19 coach from outside. As it pulled over, I could only see five or six passengers on board. More than half had their cheeks squished against the window, sound asleep.

The girl, whom I noticed carried no bags, stood up and walked onto the coach. She looked back at me and I waved half-heartedly. She cracked a smile but it didn't look like it would last. The driver checked her ticket and turned off the ignition as he went to take a bathroom break. Within a matter of minutes, he was back and the E19 was on its way out again.

I knew I'd never see her again. It was an encounter so slight and so transient, it brought to mind old ghost stories. Much like I had no proof that the coach station had existed prior to my arrival that night, I had no proof that I'd ever really seen or talked to that girl. In fact, now that the E19 had disappeared from the electronic arrivals board, I had no proof that was even a real route.

I entertained myself for a little while, thinking of how I'd spin tonight into a spooky campfire tale one day and how I'd hold friends rapt with fear and anticipation as I told them of the young and beautiful ghost in the coach station that was never really there. *But I was there*, I'll say.

I looked back at the seat where she had sat and noticed something underneath it. With nothing better to do, I went over to take a look. It was a piece of glossy paper screwed up into a very tight ball. Whoever had crumpled this had been at it for a while. I carefully unravelled it and found it was a ghoulishly illustrated anti-abortion flyer. I'd seen similar handed out in front of Family Planning Clinics back home. Much of it was in a language I didn't speak although the obligatory Bible quote was in my own. It read, *'It is the Lord who stretches out the Heavens, lays the foundation of the earth, and forms the spirit of man within Him.'* I screwed it back up and threw it in the bin where I felt it very much belonged.

I sat back down and opened the can of drink. By the time I'd reached the bottom and could feel my teeth tingle from the sugar, the E32 coach rolled out of the night and onto the concourse. The noise of its engine seemed to reverberate around the building. I stood up and strapped my rucksack back on. When the door hissed open, I showed the driver my ticket and, to my relief, he waved me onto the coach. I had no idea what time I'd reach my destination but it didn't really matter. We were in motion now.

Patrick O'Hare: King of the Freaks

·:::·

It was a muggy September evening in London and Sue Farriner's twelfth birthday. The city's enthusiasm for exotic 'novelties' was in a buoyant infancy. From the lavish Promenade of Wonders in Drury Lane to the back room of Tom Norman's shop in Whitechapel that housed the famous 'Elephant Man', these shows drew the crowds. Londoners at the end of this brutal century seemed consoled by the revolting sights of those even less fortunate than themselves.

Sue's friend John Pope was four years older and already a regular attendee of such exhibitions, thanks to his father, a doctor whose interest was strictly professional. John had mentioned that a new house of 'novelties' would open soon on the corner of Hooper Street and boasted that he would be there on its first night.

Having heard so much about these sorts of shows, it seemed unreal to Sue that one was opening up in Mile End, only a few streets away from her own home, and on her birthday too. She was tremendously excited and begged Doctor Pope to take her with them. He eventually consented and, on that muggy September night, the three of them walked through the fog towards Hooper Street.

'Do you think there will be a pig with two heads?' Sue asked Doctor Pope. 'Charlie Rivers told me that he saw one at a house in Islington and one of the heads tried to bite him. It sounds horrid!'

The doctor chuckled and replied that he did not think that they would see a two-headed pig on this occasion. 'However,' he added, 'I have heard that Mr. O'Hare has a very interesting deformed girl that he discovered in Paris, of all places, and who is quite unlike any exhibit we have seen here in London. *Trés exotique!*'

'Deformed? How?' Sue asked, eager to let her imagination run wild in anticipation of what was to come.

'Well, my dear Sue, word has it that the girl is almost completely missing a face.' The doctor paused for dramatic effect, then lightened his tone. 'Of course, I maintain a healthy scepticism. Such elaborate deformities are often mere tricks of the eye. It's wax or make-up applied by charlatans onto ordinary urchins.'

Her enthusiasm was unhampered by Doctor Pope's doubt as they arrived at the gaslit corner of Hooper Street to find a bustle of punters already assembled outside the house. It was a diverse selection of local residents. A small pack of girls from Church Lane – the ones Sue's mother would call 'unfortunate women' – wore enormous hats and chattered loudly, alongside refined gentlemen in velvet tail coats who puffed on cigarettes and tried to keep their eyes on the house. Such exhibits brought together people who would normally not socialise. It was no longer a case of whether you were rich or poor. It was normal for 'novelty'.

Sue and the Popes muscled into the bustle and craned their necks to get a look at a painted sheet of canvas that hung between two windows on the first floor of the house. The sheet was covered with lurid depictions of deformities and, written above these in garish print, the words, 'Patrick O'Hare's Monsters Myriad'.

The house itself, to Sue's surprise, was the same modest building that until recently had belonged to Pickwick's, the funeral directors. Sue had wondered why she hadn't seen Hatty Pickwick recently. They would often hold games of pitch and toss on Thomas Street, yet Hatty had not come to play in the last couple of weeks.

At first Sue thought it was because of the burns Hatty got when the two of them tried stealing hot buns from the bakery. Hatty had seized the baking tray, without realising it was fresh from the oven and ended up with two hard, jagged burns like icicles across the palms of her hands. Perhaps Mr. Pickwick now thought Sue was a bad influence. The repossession of the house, however, suggested she and her family had moved on, as was increasingly the case for small businesses in the East End. When the money stopped coming in, it was easier to pull a moonlight flit than to stay and pay off debts to the landlords. Even Sue knew that.

The door to the house, funereal black, was now propped open to reveal red velvet drapes. A gangly man with protuberant eyes stood outside, blocking the entrance and beating a dusty drum that hung from ropes around his neck.

'We are here just in time,' whispered Doctor Pope and, although he was always very proper, Sue could tell he was secretly as excited as she was. The sound of a barrel organ swelled from within the house and her stomach felt like it was flipping itself over. The show was starting. She gripped Doctor Pope's hand in fright and he smiled down at her.

'Come now, Sue, you're not going to be scared, are you?' he asked, his tone only lightly mocking her.

'No, Doctor Pope,' Sue responded with uncertainty.

'Susie is a big coward,' John Pope whispered under his breath. She shot him a glance and stuck her tongue out when his father wasn't looking.

'Ladies and gentlemen, Patrick O'Hare!' yelled the man with the protuberant eyes.

Suddenly, the velvet drapes flew open and a round gentleman in a black jacket and top hat appeared. His face was smeared with white grease paint and the shirt he wore looked tight, yellowed with sweat and ready to burst under the pressure of his bulbous belly. He began to address the audience, his voice a loud yet quivering baritone, his accent Irish and strong. When he spoke, it was entirely in doggerel.

'Ladies and gentlemen, welcome aboard / Monsters you'll find in my house by the horde / From Africa, India, Europe and, well… / Some creatures so shocking, you'll think they're from Hell!'

The barrel organ resonated on a loud, discordant note as O'Hare swept aside the drapes and vanished indoors. The word 'Hell' seemed to echo back and forth down Hooper Street.

'Right then,' began the man with the protuberant eyes. 'It's a penny to come into the Monsters Myriad. Step right up and follow Mr. O'Hare through the curtains.'

Doctor Pope paid a penny each for the three of them and they walked through the door into a hallway, crushed against the muttering throng. The floors were tiled black and white in a chequer board pattern and cheap red velvet adorned the walls. The house smelt faintly of damp. O'Hare stood directly in front of the crowd at the end of the hallway and spoke once more.

'The first room I'll show you is where you will see / The beasts that no longer breathe like you and me / I took the remains and preserved them in there / So enter the Room Of The Dead if you dare!'

Upon finishing his rhyme, he opened a door to the left and led the punters through into a drawing room. The only source of light inside was a gas lamp affixed to the wall farthest away. Sue held tighter to Doctor Pope's hand as they all edged forward.

In the gloom, to which all soon became accustomed, there were several jars of pickled creatures. The nearest one contained two foetuses, conjoined at the hip. John Pope ran his fingers along the glass jar, fascinated by its contents. Sue wished she wasn't afraid and could get that close herself.

The two children moved around the room and examined the other jars, which included a starfish with a human face and the skull of a man-eating goat. Sue didn't like to look, for fear of the skull springing to life and jumping out of the jar, but her fascination with these wondrously strange things made it nigh on impossible to turn away.

In the corner of the room stood an open coffin, pushed up against the wall. Along its uppermost rim, the word 'Pickwick' had been stamped. Inside, a man-shaped package was wrapped up in soiled bandages and propped upright, bound with straps. An official looking certificate was pinned to the coffin and claimed that this was an ancient, mummified corpse, exhumed by O'Hare (here referred to as Doctor O'Hare) on a foreign archaeological dig in 1880. Unable to resist touching something that had come from so far away, Sue reached her hand forward.

Immediately, as if materialising from the darkness, the man

with the protuberant eyes grabbed her by the wrist. His hand felt unpleasant, clammy against her skin.

'You can't touch that, young lady,' he hissed. People were now watching. The man smiled and loosened his grip. 'You might just wake 'im up. Har har.'

He winked and let go. Sue shook her head, too scared to say anything. Moving away, she stole one last glance at the coffin and she imagined the cold, fleshless corpse underneath the wrapping. A shiver ran up her spine.

Shortly afterwards, O'Hare led them back across the hallway and announced the exhibit within the next room.

'Born with a defect, she grew up too fat / Society wouldn't have any of that / A woman as big, I assure you've not seen her / So now I present to you… Obesitina!'

With this, he opened the door to a vast dining room, again decorated with chequer board tiles and velvet. In the centre of this room was an elaborately sculpted giant oyster shell containing Obesitina, the exhibition's fat lady, dressed in oversized undergarments. It was difficult, from certain angles, to even make out a recognisable shape within her slippery mass. The man with the protuberant eyes announced that audience members were allowed to move closer to Obesitina as long as they didn't touch.

The reaction of the crowd, as some of the braver amongst them stepped forward to the quivering human blubber draped across the shell, was intriguing. The girls from Church Lane whispered in evident disgust, whilst one or two of the gentlemen seemed embarrassed, sweating beneath their silk hats.

This exhibit was not as interesting to Sue as the jars had been and she could see that Doctor Pope, who shook his head in disapproval, was equally unmoved. John Pope, however, had edged closer to Obesitina and was inquisitively examining one of her elephantine legs with an awe-struck expression. All the while, the fat lady watched eerily on, her puffy red eyes being the only part of her that visibly moved beyond a quiver.

John looked almost disappointed when, after a minute or two, O'Hare ushered everyone back into the hallway, but Sue was bored and glad to be shot of the fat lady. Despite a large window being wide open in the back of the room, the air had felt stale, sticky and sickly-sweet with ghastly perfume.

From the bottom of the steps, O'Hare began to announce the next exhibit.

'From deep in the jungles, my next beast was flown / Caged - for your safety - I should make it known / Please watch his performance, I hope you enjoy / Congo The African Cannibal Boy!'

He then revealed a room at the back of the house, its doorway hidden beneath the stairs. The room was dark, with stone walls and a stone floor. In the centre of the floor was a cage containing a black-skinned dwarf and a metal trunk. Sue had never seen either a black-skinned man or a dwarf before and found Congo captivating as he paced up and down, mumbling incantations in a deep, foreign voice.

The man with protuberant eyes began to furiously beat his drum again as O'Hare revealed a wooden stick and used a gas lamp's flame to set fire to its tip. With a flamboyant gesture to the crowd, O'Hare thrust the ignited stick at the dwarf, who grabbed hold of it and plunged it into his mouth. As the crowd gasped in shock and O'Hare stepped backwards, Congo removed the now extinguished stick and blew a violent cascade of bright red sparks from his mouth into the darkness. Sue stared as this magical fire dissolved into the air and Congo roared, fixing his eyes directly on her. She screamed. There was something about those coal black eyes, embedded in that sweat-soaked ebony skin that provoked deep dread in her.

John Pope immediately laughed, which caused a ripple of giggles to erupt amongst the Church Lane girls. Sue's face flushed crimson with embarrassment while Doctor Pope ran his fingers soothingly across her head and murmured, 'There, there, Sue. He can't hurt you from inside the cage.'

Sue fought back tears as O'Hare stared straight at her with an unreadable smile on his face. When she turned back towards Congo, the dwarf's mouth was full of sodden, red raw meat.

A few of the older girls screamed this time. Congo seized another slab of the dripping meat from the metal trunk and devoured it with as much zeal as he had the first one. Sue immediately wanted to leave and could not have been more relieved when, after Congo had finished his second helping, the crowd were ushered back out to the hallway.

O'Hare now crept amongst the group and occasionally allowed a finger to casually roam across someone's shoulder or up their neck as he, with an ominous tone, announced his pride and joy; the final 'novelty' of the exhibition.

'She hears no evil, nor hears any call / She cannot speak - she sees nothing at all / Born with no face in the slums of Paris / A poor orphan girl who came somehow to me / I ask you to gaze at this pitiful child / Whose life has been robbed, like her face, of its smile / I call her Rien, make yourselves quite prepared / 'Tis time for my final display to be bared!'

Night had fallen fast outside. There was some trepidation, as the building seemed to be suddenly so much colder, but they all followed O'Hare through another door and down a filthy stone staircase into the cellar beneath the house. The further they descended, the more Sue had to fight back an urge to retch. The stench of death left over from the Pickwicks' undertaking business lingered in the air, thick and repugnant. Doctor Pope covered his nose with a handkerchief.

At the bottom of the stone steps, the cellar itself was revealed as a damp room with sawdust scattered across the floor. A gas lamp illuminated patches of green moss growing on blackened walls. Sat within a small cage on the ground, Sue could make out the spindly shadow of a young girl.

O'Hare walked across to the cage and stuck his hand inside to squeeze the girl's shoulders. The girl leapt upwards at his touch and began flinging herself wildly at the sides of the cage.

She was dressed only in two cloth rags to cover her modesty and looked normal in all respects except for one. Her face was an empty strip of bare flesh. She had no eyes, no mouth and, beneath thin, lank strands of hair, no ears either. An amorphous bump, where an ordinary person's nose would be, remained, along with two nostrils, but everything else was missing.

Involuntarily, Sue began to imagine an existence as empty as that and tears welled up in her eyes. The girl in the cage continued to fumble around and wave her hands through the bars, making a ferocious racket.

As Sue's face plunged into the safety of Doctor Pope's chest, she heard a mixed reaction from the crowd. Some towards the back jeered and laughed raucously, but most of the punters were silenced with shock. Sue caught a glimpse of John Pope's face. The ever-present rosy glow in his cheeks had faded to ghostly white. Even Doctor Pope stared at the girl in the cage with his forehead creased and mouth slackly open in disbelief. He eventually feigned a nervous laugh and said, 'Oh, come now, Sue, anyone can see it's just make-up. A trick of the eye.'

※ ※ ※

Afterwards, the crowd filed out of the exhibition and into Hooper Street. Sue overheard their conversations. Some were openly sceptical of the girl's authenticity, while others exchanged horrified expletives and stuttered in amazement.

Doctor Pope walked Sue and John back to Thomas Street and none of them said a word throughout the journey. John still looked pale and his father seemed lost in his own thoughts. When they reached Sue's home, she thanked the doctor for taking her to the exhibition and bade him goodnight, returning to the care of her mother.

Although put to bed immediately, Sue could not sleep. Her thoughts were plagued by images of Rien. The notion of such a black, silent existence was mortifying. 'Anyone can see it's just make-up,' Doctor Pope had insisted but did he really believe that? Did Sue, for that matter? She became determined to find out for herself. The only way she could rest would be to know that this poor, wretched girl and her awful fate were not real. Sue knew she must return to the house on Hooper Street. Praying that the window in the fat lady's drawing room was still going to be wide open, she silently slipped her shoes on and slid out through the front door into the foggy London midnight.

Despite the walk to Hooper Street only lasting a minute or two, it stretched out unbearably. Flickering shadows danced within the fog, across the walls and atop the cobblestones. Each step through the miasma reminded Sue that this was certainly not an appropriate time or place for a twelve-year-old girl to be out walking. The now bitter air nipped at her skin. She could almost feel criminal hands reaching out from the darkness to grab her but it was just her imagination. The streets were mercifully quiet.

When at last she reached the house, Sue found the drawing room window had indeed remained open. With caution, she pulled it as wide as it would go and sneaked through, carefully dropping to the floor with a soft thud. Obesitina was asleep in her oyster shell chair, snoring heavily.

Creeping past the fat lady, Sue reached the hallway and tried hard not to look at the door by the staircase, the one that led to the African Cannibal Boy's room. The sight of his hateful anthracite stare flashed through her mind and she felt her breath come shorter. Hardly daring to exhale, for fear the house might hear her, she tiptoed through the cellar door and began to carefully walk the stairs.

Once more Sue felt the urge to retch. She entered the cellar and saw the gas lamp was still lit. Rien was awake. The faceless girl crawled on the floor of her cage and occasionally bumped her body into the sides. Sue approached her and, shakily, pushed her hand through the bars. Her fingertips explored Rien's face and then recoiled as she realised with certainty that this was no cheap make-up trick. The strip of flesh above where the girl's nose should have been was moist with sweat and Sue felt the veins behind it pulsate. Rien flung herself backward across the cage, her arms flailing in confused panic.

Sue did not know what to do. She could hear a ragged wheeze from the girl's nostrils and when Sue looked down, she noticed something even more horrifying. Two hard, jagged burns like icicles across the palms of Rien's hands.

'Hatty?' Sue gasped.

All of a sudden, she felt a familiar clammy palm clamp down on her wrist. As she spun round to see the man with the protuberant eyes, her other wrist was grabbed by Congo, the black-skinned dwarf.

She screamed and screamed until Patrick O'Hare emerged from the inky murk of the cellar, his white painted face glowing. He spoke once more in rhyme. His voice was deeper and gruffer than before, almost inhuman.

'Now it is time for this lass to receive / A punishment fitting the crime, I believe / A curious girl with too much to see / Will soon be the finest O'Hare novelty.'

His eyes blazed as he produced a handful of shimmering red dust from his pocket and blew it in Sue's face. She saw sparks, felt a searing pain across the skin of her face and immediately fainted.

When she awoke, there was just the blackness, the silence and the need to scream. Yet she could not.

Sue would never know but soon it would be time for her and Hatty to be moved on to a larger, more prestigious house; one where their new identity would properly come of age and they would become the most popular and horrifying 'novelties' of their time. *Ladies and gentlemen, Patrick O'Hare presents Rien and Blanca, The Famous Cypher Sisters!*

Duplicity

∴

I've always thought of myself as one of the good guys. Now, I'll admit that no one these days can be a saint but I think I have an above average code of morals. I was brought up to know the difference between right and wrong and I've always tried to avoid hurting other people where possible.

So one thing I never would've expected I could do would be to live with someone – and by live I mean share their bed, their body, their soul – and yet all the while be in love with someone else entirely. I know, right? I thought this was the kind of thing reserved for love rats in bad soap operas or for heartless weirdoes that couldn't feel love in the first place. But no. It can happen even to the good guys.

I am in love with Emily. Yet I am also in love with Claire.

Some history:

Emily and I met during our first year at UCL. She was studying philosophy and I was taking business and economics so you'd've maybe thought our paths wouldn't cross much. As it happened, we just met by chance in the canteen one wet afternoon. Everybody wanted to get in from the rain, which had just sprung itself on us, so it was rammed with other students. There wasn't much space. She had an empty seat next to her so I took it. We started chatting.

She struck me as a gentle sort; soft-spoken and kind of

fragile. I wanted to scoop her up in my arms and hide her in my coat. I probably could have done just that too, she was so tiny and delicate. When I asked her if she'd want to meet up some time for a drink, she got all shy. She closed curtains of blonde hair across gorgeous pale blue eyes and wouldn't let me see her blushing. I could see she was smiling though. I fell in love.

We dated for the rest of our time at UCL and, when we were both done with Uni, we moved in together properly. Our first place was small; a nasty old studio flat in Clerkenwell that had damp on the walls and, before long, rats. I left little piles of poison on the kitchen floor and, each morning, would wake up and find the bodies lying there. I'd chuck them away with one hand while drinking my morning coffee with the other. It was pretty grim and no way to live, right? But I knew it'd only be temporary. Needs must and all that.

Within a month or so, my business degree and a couple of good interviews landed me a foot in the door at HBG Telecoms. The money was good so Emily and I were able to move out of Clerkenwell and into a two-bedroom place on the far reaches of the Piccadilly Line, all the way out in Zone 3. The flat was much nicer and the commuting was alright. Things were looking up.

Then tragedy struck. A few weeks after we'd moved into the new flat, Emily's parents were both killed in a house fire. One of those things you hear about but don't think could ever happen to you or anyone you know. But it did. I guess Emily was already more susceptible than most to bouts of misery but something like this was horrible by any standards. She just lost it completely and before long she was housebound with her depression. She wouldn't go out, not even to the corner shop, so I continued to support the pair of us. I didn't mind – I mean, not considering what she'd gone through – but after a few months of it, I started to miss having fun. Pleasure was outlawed within the flat and I was getting frustrated.

So while I spent most nights looking after Emily and helping her get through her grief, I began to go out socially once a week after work. Just a little release valve from all the pressure, you know? A swift few drinks with some old friends from Uni who were also working in the city.

One of these old friends was Claire. Now, I'd met Claire when I first started my degree and I'd fancied her right off the bat. She had a sharp, cat-like face with huge almond eyes and full, soft lips that she loved to paint shocking red. Her jet-black hair bobbed around the base of her chin and she had a knockout figure; curvy in all the right places, if you know what I mean. But back then, it didn't go beyond a bit of a crush. I'd lost interest in Claire when she started dating my friend Rob. It went against my moral code entirely to have designs on a mate's girlfriend and, around the same time, I'd met Emily anyway so it was a moot point. Claire and I stayed casual friends and my previous feelings towards her never resurfaced or got in the way.

So anyhow, we started hanging out again for drinks and somehow one of these sessions ended up with just me and Claire on our own in the pub. I don't know how. Usually there were more of us but you know how these things go. Especially if the weather's bad or whatever. We started off with awkward small talk but, as the night went on and we drank more, we loosened up. After a while, the chat moved on to relationships and I told her all about Emily's recent troubles. Claire sympathised. Turns out she'd lost her own mum years back and she never even knew her dad. She had no real family to speak of any more and I think it got to her. I mumbled 'sorry' and tried to change the subject, asking her how Rob was, and that was when things got interesting. Turns out they'd recently split up and, at that point, I started to see Claire in a different light again. She was suddenly available.

We carried on chatting but I found my attention wandering from the conversation and onto her body. I would steal the odd glimpse of her cleavage or, when she stood up to go to the bar, follow her backside with my eyes, gazing at the tease of it beneath the black leather mini-skirt. Now she was single, it was as if a switch had been flicked in my brain: she was fair game. It barely even crossed my mind that *I* was involved in another relationship altogether.

Nothing happened but the next morning, I felt awful, sick from guilt and booze. I tried convincing myself that I'd just been drunk and horny and that there was nothing to worry about but it didn't work. I couldn't stop thinking about Claire. I needed to see her again. I wondered if she felt the same way and began fantasising about us being together. It shot my concentration to bits, at work and home.

Before I could really stop myself, I just stepped back and let my lust drive the situation forwards. Soon, Claire and I began meeting one another by ourselves a couple of times a week in the pub next to my office and I began lying to Emily. I'd toss off casual remarks like, 'Oh, do you remember Claire and Rob from college? I'm meeting them both for drinks.' Of course Emily remembered them but she had no idea about either my secret crush or the fact that Rob and Claire were no longer together, let alone the fact that I was just meeting Claire by herself.

I felt guilty about the lies but kept telling myself it was acceptable because nothing wrong was actually happening outside of my fantasies. I was still sticking to my code. Claire and I were totally just friends, even though I was, if I'm honest, getting the distinct impression that she too wanted more. It was there in the way her eyes would meet mine sometimes across the table. I could read them like a dirty book. She was interested alright.

Of course, code or no code, I knew that the second Claire actually said 'yes', I wouldn't even blink before jumping on her. I wanted her so badly, so physically, that it was too strong to be held back by feelings. On the days when we were meant to meet, I'd spend time cleaning myself in the bathroom at work and praying that tonight would be the night when Claire and I would go back to her flat together.

My sex life with Emily was okay, I suppose. We had a few months where nothing happened but, after a while, her libido came back, although we were never particularly wild. It got to the point where, as much as I tried not to, I would be thinking of Claire. It would be Claire's breasts I was caressing, Claire's soft lips I was kissing and Claire's name I'd come dangerously close to whispering while with Emily.

For some reason, I kept thinking of the lyrics to that old Dolly Parton song and especially the line about the guy talking about Jolene in his sleep, calling her name while poor old Dolly lay next to him trying not to cry. Do people really do that, I wondered? Talk in their sleep about the girls they fancy? Either way, it got me paranoid and soon I couldn't bear to sleep at all, in case I gave my secret feelings away and hurt Emily. It wasn't good. My health suffered. Even Claire said one time that she'd noticed the dark circles under my eyes, something I berated myself for, as it was hardly an attractive quality.

I wondered how I'd managed to so quickly blur my affections. I swapped the love I'd felt for Emily onto Claire and yet still had feelings towards Emily. As a naturally monogamous kind of guy, this was all new territory and I didn't like it. See, Emily was a beautiful girl and I was lucky to have her. Besides, it wasn't like I could just leave her, was it? Not in her state. But whenever I closed my eyes or let my mind wander, it was Claire I was thinking of and Claire's daily routine I was contemplating; working out where she was, what she was doing, what she was wearing - or not wearing as the case may be. Emily was too familiar. I knew exactly what she'd be doing at any given time and it was boring. It didn't ever cross my mind. I guess it's easy to get a bit ho-hum after so long in a relationship but I was burning for someone whose ways, whose thoughts and whose body were all a mystery, waiting to be excitedly unveiled.

The turning point came one night in the pub, when Claire admitted she could no longer afford to live in the flat that she and Rob had rented together. He'd long moved out and she just couldn't pay the rent all by herself. She was stressed about it and told me how much she hated looking for flats and how everywhere even half-decent in London was way outside of her price range. She mentioned again that she had no family to move in with and then said she didn't even have any friends she felt comfortable enough around for a flat share. It was heartbreaking. Without even thinking twice about how Emily would feel, I offered Claire the spare bedroom in our flat.

It's been two and a half weeks now since I moved Claire in and I admit that I'm not proud of some of the things I've had to do. The temptation of Claire under the same roof was too much to bear and I've been sleeping with her on an almost nightly basis since she got here. Emily hasn't got a clue about it and Claire hasn't shown any signs of guilt over what we're doing. It puts my mind at rest that emotions aren't flaring and everybody's getting along.

It's got pretty intense though. There have been nights when I've sneaked out of Claire's room after we've made love and then gone to Emily and slept with her too which, on the surface, probably sounds awful. But come on, sometimes we can all do a bad thing or two in the throes of desire and God knows I desire both of them so much right now.

When I did the very bad thing I had to do in order to make all this work, it was easier than I thought it'd be. I already had the poison from the old Clerkenwell flat and there's not that much difference between laying it on the floor or dropping some in a drink really, is there? It's the same principle. Not nice to think about but needs must and all that. It was a means to an end and the end's worked out well for us, even if I do say so myself.

I sometimes find myself wondering how different this arrangement of ours would be if either girl were still alive but then I tell myself that it's better this way. No one has to get hurt any more. There are no more lies. No more tears. No matter which girl I've spent the night beside, I can still look at myself in the mirror before heading off to work and know that I'm doing my best. It's a bad old world but at least I'm still one of the good guys, right?

Emerson's Last Stand, or, Keeping Up With The Joneses

·:⁙:·

George Emerson nervously inhaled the crisp air of the grey November afternoon and shivered as he saw the looming stone gate of the bridge. A large number of people were already gathered along the path, cheering loudly with the kind of raucous excitement that the town of Monmouth sees but once a year.

Mr. Emerson's partner, Mary Simmons, stood beside him, discreetly attired in a dress of grey delaine, her silvery-blonde hair tucked up beneath her bonnet. He glanced at her and his heart began pumping faster as he realised how much was at stake today. She cracked a slow but warm smile, attempting to reassure him; this tall, broad-shouldered man with bushy brown whiskers and fire in his chestnut eyes whose face had become meek as a lamb's since last night.

'Don't be nervous, Mrs. Simmons,' he said to her from the corner of his mouth. He was barely audible above the whispery noises of the wind. 'We're going to win this.'

Mrs. Simmons offered a brief nod of reassurance although she realised his words meant little. 'Of course we are, Mr. Emerson.'

The previous night, they had both sat rigid in the perfumed parlour of Korben Crain, a noted local Spiritualist whom they had consulted for guidance. The clairvoyant had performed a number of mind-reading tricks with playing cards and then gazed into his crystal ball to predict the worst. In spite of the partnership's unbroken series of wins this year, Crain informed them without ambiguity that today's all-important game would be lost to their opponents, the Joneses.

The annual final of Monmouth's bridge-whist tournament had been a tradition held on the town's stone bridge since the mid-16th century, come rain or shine. Bridge on the bridge. Now, over two hundred years since its inception, it still remained a highlight of the town's calendar. The atmosphere every November 1st was one of anticipation and fierce competition as the two highest scoring teams from the year's tournament squared off against one another beneath the gate of the town's ancient and most imposing structure.

Mr. Llewelyn, mercurial landlord at the Murder of Ravens, had brought out two-dozen barrels of his special bridge-whist ale. The Owen sisters from the local haberdashery had made cucumber sandwiches, an especial treat for the children of the town. Mrs. Lewis, the butcher's wife, had cooked her famous mutton stew that now sat steaming at the edge of the bridge in a giant pot, ready for eager eaters to help themselves. Many of the townsfolk liked to bring something of their own and now all were lined up along the bridge and its surrounding woodland, chattering excitedly and peddling their wares.

Mr. Emerson and Mrs. Simmons stepped onto the bridge and walked up to the stone gate, where they were greeted with applause from their friends and supporters. They shook hands with the Joneses, who were already at the table, and sat down. The table looked as beautiful and powerful as ever, its ornate mahogany legs glistening in the low sun. Throughout the year it was kept locked beneath the church with the rest of the apparatus for the final. Crowther, the local vicar and traditional games master, was fluttering around the table, greeting the players with a creaking smile that flashed firebrand teeth.

The crowd roared suddenly. Emerson spun around to see a large carriage bearing the Duke of Monmouth's livery. The coachman reined in the horses and a manservant hurried to the side of the car to allow the Duke and Duchess to step down. Both of them looked resplendent in new costumes from London specifically designed for the occasion. The Duchess' velvet dress was embroidered with the patterns of playing card suits and the Duke wore an unusual chiffon hat in the shape of a black spade.

Emerson knew that the arrival of the Duke meant that the game could at last begin. He took one more look at Mrs. Simmons and silently prayed to the Spirits for guidance in the game. As Crowther the vicar sat down, Mr. Jones shuffled the first deck of cards, passed them across the table for Emerson to cut and flashed a snide grin that spread all the way across his leathery, vulture-like face. Crowther began to deal the cards, thirteen to each player, revealing the ace of clubs as the opening trump.

The chatter of the crowd at the end of the bridge put Emerson's concentration in jeopardy and he played a nervous, overcautious first trick that was lost to the Joneses. Luckily, Mrs. Simmons managed to put down the highest card in the second trick and although there was no trump, the hand was theirs.

By the end of the eleventh trick, Emerson was sweating profusely, in spite of the cold weather, and could barely hear anything above the swirling noise of the wind and the crowd, that had turned into an indistinguishable cacophony in his ears. He knew bridge-whist inside out and he knew he was playing dismally. With so much pressure to win the final, his strategies were falling to pieces and his concentration kept floating across to Korben Crain's predictions, to Mrs. Simmons beside him and to how this would now probably be the last time they would be able to play together.

As the thirteenth and final trick wound up with a well-placed king of hearts from Mrs. Simmons, Crowther began the scoring process. The Joneses were declared winners, having reached five points over the allotted six before Emerson and Simmons had even accrued two. After the Duke and Duchess came to shake hands with all four players, the game was officially over. The crowd went wild. The two losers found themselves seized by a pair of burly draymen from the Murder of Ravens.

As they were led towards the large wooden winding wheel erected by the side of the bridge, Emerson heard the voice of Mr. Jones congratulating him on a good game and felt sturdy old rope tying his hands behind his back. The noise of the crowd reached a feverish new level as the draymen fastened Emerson into a leather harness and Mary Simmons into a separate one nearby. Emerson became disorientated and nauseous. He panicked, though not for what was being done to him; after all, it was Monmouth tradition and a risk undertook whenever one began playing bridge-whist. Instead, the bubbling sickness in his stomach was caused by the pressure to say the things that could soon no longer be said.

'Mrs. Simmons,' he began hoarsely, as the harness tightened and a drayman lifted him up to the ledge of the bridge. 'I.. I.. I want you to know, I have always cared a great deal for you.'

'I do know, George,' she replied with a tired smile as the other drayman lifted her up alongside her playing partner. 'I do know.'

As the wooden wheel began to creak around slowly, Emerson looked back at the crowd with a renewed sense of clarity. The Duke and Duchess were dancing widdershins in a circle round the table with the Joneses, as the butcher's boy played a lively jig on his violin. Emerson closed his eyes and listened to the sounds around him, becoming clearer with each inch he was lowered down off the bridge, within the harness; the crunching of cucumbers between children's teeth; the stamp of dancing feet on stone; the upbeat melody of the violin; the sloshing of ale in the barrels; the lighting of torches as the evening began to fall; the laughter of revelling townsfolk; the steady pulsing of his heartbeat; the splash as his body plunged into the water; the deep inhalation of his last breath of air…

In Every Dream Home A Heartache

⋰

We never wanted to have a child. This was a fundamental fact of our relationship. You could probably argue it was even what brought us together.

In the early eighties, the East Village was alive with like-minded freaks, queers and misfits. When I first opened the Birdhouse - a converted apartment in a 1st Avenue dive for transgressive artists to show off their work and party the night away in a chemical blur of coke and vodka - it seemed like we'd live that way forever. There was a circle of us, a scene if you will, united by the prospect of expressing our displeasure through art so distasteful that few other galleries would've considered even looking at it, let alone exhibiting it.

We all came from different backgrounds and teased one another over any distinguishing features. We gave each other nicknames like Cowboy, The Twins, Roly-Poly, Batshit and Sketch. Anna was known as Moneypenny, on account of the fact that she was a trust-fund baby. We kind of hated her for that, as the rest of us scrabbled around for cash-in-hand jobs while waiting and praying for a rich patron. She grew angry whenever we called her out on it though, as she desperately wanted to be taken seriously as an artist and everyone knows that only the poor, desperate or crazy can create anything with true meaning.

The irony was that, out of us all, Anna probably stood the most chance of actually getting somewhere with her art on its own merit. Her first show at the Birdhouse was a series of paintings called 'Solitary In Menstrual Night' that was as savage as it was beautiful. I think we all coasted off her talent for a while after that, believing that as soon as Anna was discovered, our collective success would follow as naturally as night follows day. All we had to do was keep drinking, keep partying and wait.

It didn't happen. We didn't work hard enough for it. Almost every night at the Birdhouse culminated in orgiastic excess to the extent that it became intimidating for anyone who wasn't one of us to even come near us. Serious critics and patrons would go to the Now Gallery or 8BC. The parties there, though infamous, were put to shame by our Bacchanalian pursuit of oblivion.

We all fucked each other in those days. Men with men, women with men, women with women, it didn't matter. Restrictions on anything, sexuality included, were for the birds. I know I must've fucked Anna several times at those parties but couldn't tell you where, how, on which nights or who else was involved. Luckily, like all the girls there, she was on the pill. Having children was anti-art, as far as we were all concerned. We naively co-opted the queer term 'breeders' to talk of the ones who weren't as free and smart as us because they bought into the fallacy of procreation.

But of course, things changed. We all clung on to the dream of being artists but the parties decreased in frequency and our work grew safer. Although no one spoke of it, we began to feel a mutual sense of regret that we'd alienated just about everyone else in the art scene through our extremity. I watched as even the most flamboyant personalities, like Sketch and Batshit, started to gradually spend more time and energy on their dull nine to five jobs than they did on their art. Some of them disappeared from the scene entirely, only to resurface a little later at a Birdhouse party to bore us all senseless with non-stories about working life. There were two reasons they came back, as far as I could tell. The first was a delusion that they were still somehow interesting or relevant. The second was that they liked to look down on those of us who remained tied to this dead-end life. No one spoke it aloud but one question was always there in the way they looked at me and at Anna: *Haven't you grown out of this yet?*

The Twins, Emma and Alex (who weren't actually related), were the first to breed. When Emma got pregnant, she came to the Birdhouse and announced it in front of us all. Anna's immediate response was to suggest an abortion party. I laughed but Emma failed to see the funny side, telling us all gravely that she and Alex were delighted about it and that they were going to have the baby. The rest of the conversations that evening had The Twins on the defensive, continually protesting that they hadn't 'sold out' and that they'd raise their child to be a great artist one day.

Something changed in Emma when she gave birth though. Gone was the peroxide mohawk and black leather. She grew out her naturally curled brown hair and began wearing tie-dye dresses. Whenever I ran into her around the Village, on her way to Wholefoods or some such nightmare, she'd be carrying the baby in a papoose and I hardly recognized her. I always had to look twice before saying hello. She'd been one of the most highly-strung of all of us but now possessed an eerie calm. She was someone's mom and that was the end of that. As the decade progressed, a stream of new life and new death divided us. The Twins had opened the floodgates on breeding and now everyone wanted to ride the wave. Couples formed. More babies. On the dark flip side, several of our circle were claimed by AIDS. With hindsight, it was a surprise that any of us escaped that particular fate, something that can be attributed to stone-blind luck.

By the tail end of the eighties, the scene had flatlined. Although the surviving ones all kept in touch and had parties at the Birdhouse every now and then, it was different. Most of the revellers would settle for a glass or two of red wine. Those with children would bring the crying, shitting bastards along and, even when they didn't, the anecdotes would be there. I began to know more by proxy about the consistency of infant faeces than I ever wanted to know. It was mind numbing.

So Anna and I came together because we were the only two left who weren't dead or, worse yet, parents. Instead we clung vainly to our dreams. I still kept the Birdhouse running but spent most of my days alone in an empty room, putting together archives of photos and texts from its glory days. I held to the thought that one day someone would walk in and decide that a retrospective was in order, then suddenly New York would wake up to what had been under its nose the whole time. I got money from a gig writing dispatches from the East Coast art scene for a trendy Californian magazine but this just made me depressed. Writing about the successes of others while my own gallery failed and rotted away into obscurity was a painful reminder that I'd squandered my thirty-five years on the planet and had no idea how I'd spend whatever I had left.

Anna continued painting but the fire she'd had was gone. She became addicted to the thrill of a sale and, rather than expressing herself purely, began painting to order. At some point in the mid-eighties, there'd been a run on tacky paintings of the Manhattan skyline. Anna rattled off some of these, largely as a joke, but received both moderate acclaim and more sales than ever before. After that, she painted series after series of skylines, even after the interest had dried up, desperate to replicate the success, to have others tell her she was worthy; that she was good. She obviously didn't need the money. She just wanted to feel as if there was some kind of meaning in her life.

After falling into bed one too many times in 1990, it became apparent we were starting a relationship, so we began renting an apartment in Greenwich Village together, above a convenience store. Our life in coupledom was as happy as it could be, considering it was built on our shared sense of abject failure. We had perfunctory sex every now and again and it was good. There's no such thing as bad sex, after all. We bought groceries together, we slept in each other's arms and we struggled to stay focused on our art, as the threat of dead-eyed comfort swaddled us in its lacklustre temptations. I stopped dying my hair black and dressed more for comfort than style. Anna clung on to her severe hairdo, which once made her look like a white redheaded Grace Jones, but she was approaching an age where it was becoming more embarrassing than hip.

With the Birdhouse parties being so boring now, Anna and I made a point of going to a Lower East Side dive bar once in a while and getting shitfaced. We'd get into fights with barflies and argue fiercely about everything from art to politics with anyone who'd listen. If no one would listen, we'd argue with each other. It made us feel young again, just being able to release all that anger. One night, she punched me in the face so hard, I split my lip open. With blood pouring down my shirt, I dragged her into an alleyway and we fucked like we hadn't fucked since the early eighties. When I sobered up the next morning, it scared me. What were we becoming? We couldn't fight our own irrelevance. We had absorbed the sporadic, impotent rage of the breeders; of the normals.

The night we met Tilly, we were staggering back home drunk after one of these nights. No one had been punched or fucked that night; we'd spent most of it trying to outdo each other on who was the most righteous and artistically pure. We'd worked ourselves up such that we both believed that somehow we were making the world a better place with our open-minded independence. We sometimes liked to talk ourselves up like that, to avoid facing the reality of our limitless self-pity.

When we got to the apartment, a small child was sitting outside. She had blood on her shirt and was crying. I looked at Anna. Although neither of us really knew how to talk to children, we couldn't just leave her there. She was no more than three or four years old and it was a cold night. She looked so helpless and tiny and insubstantial, like she'd blow away if we didn't shelter her from the wind. More importantly, if we'd walked away we'd have felt far too hypocritical, having only recently established what great saints we were.

'Who the fuck would leave a fucking kid here?' slurred Anna, put out by the sheer inconvenience of this crying, bloodstained creature shivering on the doorstep.

'We should call the cops.' I noted.

At that point, the child looked up at me expectantly. 'Help,' she croaked. Her green eyes were wet and her hair matted, possibly with blood. She was pale and pretty but had definitely seen better days.

'Where's your mom and dad, kid?' I asked.

She just shook her head and started crying again.

'Mom? Dad?' I repeated, wondering if she was old or smart enough to understand even these simple words.

'Let's get her inside,' Anna said. 'It's freezing.'

'Really?' the child asked, proving she could speak after all. 'I can come in?'

'Of course you can. Of course you can,' I said, scooping her up in my arms and sealing all of our fates. She smelled like a butcher's shop and I worried that I might throw up the quart of vodka I'd put away that evening.

Anna unlocked the door and I carried the child upstairs without puking.

'I'm Tilly,' the child said, wiping her eyes.

'Tilly? Well, hello. I'm Adam. This is Anna.' I might've belched at this point. I was a mess.

'Hello.' Tilly waved her tiny hand.

As we crossed the threshold, into the apartment, the feeling hit me. Tilly had taken control. We were at her command. It's difficult to explain the feeling of being controlled by another's mind. I could still think. I was still very much myself but certain judgements that I would've made normally just wouldn't form. A wall would spring up. Decisions of any importance were not my own. I knew I could still pick which cereal to eat for breakfast by myself but much of how I'd spend my time from there on was dictated wordlessly by Tilly, whose thoughts took residence somewhere in the back of my mind.

It happened to Anna as well. As soon as Tilly was inside the apartment, neither of us spoke again about calling the police. If we'd been thinking independently, this would've been the first thing we'd have done. It was not only irrational but completely illegal to just harbour a child you found on the street. But Tilly had already begun to work on us. Our minds were tuned in to blank obedience.

Together, Anna and I walked Tilly to the bathroom, took her out of her clothes and bathed her. She no longer seemed as traumatized as she had before. She giggled as we sponged her. When she was all cleaned up, Anna wrapped her up in an adult-sized kimono and I marvelled aloud at what a beautiful child she was. Even as I said it, I knew it was strange. I'd often thought I had some kind of biological deficiency in that I failed to react to children with anything beyond a mild unease. Yet now, as I looked at Tilly, laughing at her own absurdity as she was swallowed by Anna's kimono, I was overcome with love and affection; a desire to protect her at all costs.

The first few weeks with Tilly passed like hours. Anna and I still washed and ate regularly like we used to but beyond that, we did little except serve Tilly. I didn't even consider going to the Birdhouse. Instead, we blew what was left of Anna's trust fund on decorating our spare room – previously her studio – like a nursery and buying clothes and toys for Tilly's amusement. Gradually our hours shifted and we began to exist, as a family, only by night. We slept in the daytime. Every few days, Tilly would get sick. Real sick. She'd turn ashen and her eyes would sink a little into her skull. She'd cough up dust and cry until one of us went out to fetch her medicine.

If I'd been in possession of my own mind, I would've responded with horror to sneaking along the darkest alleys of the Bowery in the small hours but instead, it just seemed natural. I thought nothing as I slit the first bum's throat and held an empty vodka bottle to the wound, watching as it filled in seconds with the crimson tincture that Tilly required. There was a time when I'd've known these bums. We used to often invite them into the Birdhouse during our parties back in the day, ply them with booze and quiz them about their life stories for fun. But now I didn't recognize any of them. That said, even if I had done, I still wouldn't have hesitated to murder them. The idea that they were fellow human beings with families somewhere, with stories to tell, with thoughts in their mind, was suppressed. My focus remained true to my duties.

After a few months of this initial control, Tilly's grip on our minds eased up. I remember waking to the spring sunshine one morning, looking at Anna and laughing for the first time in months. It was a laugh of relief. I felt a little more like myself again. I could tell that Tilly was starting to trust us more. She knew that our love and devotion for her now ran so deeply that we would serve her of our own volition. She was right.

Slowly, our personalities returned but the murderous night work became a task as mundane as running downstairs to the store for milk. Anna began painting again, some of her most beautiful work to date. Portraiture of Tilly in all her splendour, naturally. I decided to set up a show at the Birdhouse and invite the old gang. It felt like something to be proud of. Not only would Anna's paintings blow them all away but we'd be able to show off Tilly, to show them that we too had the capacity to care for another human being. We were grown-ups now. Artists and grown-ups. It was the best of both worlds.

We concocted the story that we'd adopted her from a children's home and it worked like a dream. Artists, grown-ups and philanthropists to boot. We elicited coos of sympathy and pride all round. The Twins showed up with their offspring and talked down to us, offering congratulations in a sing-song voice. We were like them now. The kids all played together and everyone admired Anna's art, remarking that although it had lost its anger it had taken on a new depth and maturity that made it wonderful. 'That'll be motherhood for you, I bet,' joked Emma, trying to keep her manic crawling offspring on its reins.

It was unanimous that the night was the best we'd all had in ages and that we simply must do it again. Even Roly-Poly had a good time. Poor Roly had been haunted by death for some time, being the last queer left in our little circle. While friends and even former lovers were dropping dead from the disease, Roly just kept on going, totally clean. He was always a little pudgy but it felt as if, with his peers withering around him, he was somehow soaking up the weight they were losing. By 1990, he looked like a big red beach ball. He still tried to maintain the image he'd always had of being a jolly old queen but his smiles usually felt false. That night, however, I watched him laughing and playing with Tilly and saw a glimpse of how he used to be. I slapped him on the back affectionately, some time late in the evening, but with the flurry of air kisses and delicate hugs that finished off the evening, I didn't get a chance to say goodbye.

Weeks passed in contentment. I would often take Tilly to work with me throughout the night at the Birdhouse where she would sit for hours painting and drawing in a sketchpad she never let me see. I didn't know why at the time but she even stopped getting sick so frequently and I no longer had to prowl the Bowery after midnight. Things were good.

It was during one of these quiet nights at the Birdhouse - some time around 4am or so - that I lost a silkscreen I'd been working on and had to go searching. I unlocked the door to the store cupboard that I rarely had reason to enter and, for a moment, returned vividly to my senses. I screamed in horror, faced with Roly-Poly hanging by his hands from the light fixture. Surrounding Roly's dangling body were twenty or so canvases of Anna's bland, unsold Manhattan skylines. It would've almost seemed comical but the state he was in robbed the situation of any levity.

His skin was a bloodless white and his body had taken on a vile, inhuman shape. He was no longer fat. I could see the bones of his ribcage but little pockets of flab still bulged out at unusual angles. His skin was covered in scabs, scars, dried bloodstains and cuts. Worst of all, he was alive. His eyes were crusted with some kind of yellow mucus but, as he saw me, they shot open and wordlessly begged me to release him. He tried to say something but it came out as just a dry, incoherent rasp.

Just then, Tilly appeared behind me.

'How could you…?' I asked, turning to face her.

'I did it for you, daddy,' she said, smiling sweetly. It was always unusual talking to her in private. She spoke in the voice of a very young child, lisping toothlessly, but could communicate in adult language. It was continually disarming.

'What?' I was aghast. 'This man is my friend, Tilly!'

'I didn't want you to have to keep going out for me. I know

you don't like it. I haven't been sick, have I, daddy? I've been a good girl.'

'You've not been sick, no, but… Jesus Christ, look at him.'

'I've been a good girl,' she said, petulantly, her face turning sour.

I turned once more to face Roly. He rasped again.

'We have to kill him,' I pleaded. 'I can't let him suffer like this.'

'You can't kill him,' she snapped, stamping her little feet. 'He's got weeks left in him. I did this for you, daddy. For you!'

Roly's body made a horrific farting noise and he groaned quietly. As a foetid smell hit my nostrils, I knew I was going to be sick and made a run for the bathroom. After vomiting for several minutes, I sat on the toilet seat, head in hands, wondering what to do. It didn't take long to realise that Tilly was testing me. She wasn't exercising her control over my thoughts now. She was forcing me to make the decision myself. Would I finish Roly's life or would I let Tilly continue to feed off him indefinitely? Who was more important? My friend or my child?

I had no doubt that Tilly would've also tested Anna in this same way. I'd noticed that recently the two of them had been bonding a lot more at home, siding against me sometimes in little family arguments. I wondered if perhaps Tilly was going to choose only one of us to be her companion. She would, of course, pick the strongest. I knew I wanted that to be me.

I stood and looked in the mirror, contemplating the situation. My reflection stared back as a sad, aged version of how I saw myself. I hated that my hairline seemed to recede a few centimetres backwards each birthday. I hated the dark circles and the wrinkles under my eyes. I hated the pallor of my skin, the way it had started to hang loose on the sides of my face, threatening to turn at any moment into jowls. I hated that I'd become exactly what I always feared. Old. Irrelevant. Normal. Invisible. That was why Anna and I stuck to the worst dive bars, where we were the youngest and the least pathetic ones there. We secretly couldn't bear the thought of going somewhere artsy or somewhere fashionable and being completely ignored by the young. The ones who still had hope for the future and had no use for the likes of us.

I wasn't ready to surrender. My time to shine hadn't come yet and it wouldn't ever if I continued to wallow like this. I wanted to be like Tilly. Immortal. Ageless. Flawless. I didn't care what the price was. I wanted to be her companion; the one she turned. With eternal youth would come power, relevance, success. I had to show no mercy.

I washed my face and returned to the store cupboard where Tilly was delicately making an incision in Roly's thigh. She'd had to stand on some boxes to even reach that far. A sliver of blood trickled out and she put her tiny mouth to it, slurping it up as Roly rasped and hissed in agony. As she heard me enter, she turned to face me. Her lips were stained deep red. She looked like she'd been trying on her mother's lipstick.

'Fine. You can keep the old cunt,' I said. 'Do what you like. Oh, and the sun'll be up in an hour. We need to go home.'

She clapped her hands together in excitement. 'Yay! Daddy! Yay!'

I closed the door and let her finish feeding, trying to think only of my own future and not about Roly. Weeks passed and eventually he gave up the ghost. I packed what little remained of him into a trash bag and threw it in the East River. Throughout this period, I grew impatient with Tilly. I'd completed my test. I'd let her torture and drink from one of my best friends. Why was she still pursuing this ridiculous game of happy families? In my mind, I convinced myself it was time for us to get rid of Anna and for Tilly to make me one of her own.

Whenever Tilly and Anna were together alone, I was suspicious and paranoid. Were they planning against me? Had Anna been tested in the same way as I had? Did she know about Roly? These questions kept me awake during the days while the girls slept. I became agitated and couldn't eat properly. It was in this state when I reached my epiphany.

I didn't need Tilly. I knew what she was. I'd seen enough movies, read enough books. Her condition was all about blood. She needed blood to live and she used her blood to turn others into creatures like herself. I was going to remove the middleman; go straight to the vein. One morning after sunrise, I slipped out of the apartment and walked to the drug store to buy hypodermics, a tourniquet and a syringe. I was surprised how much the brightness hurt my eyes. I'd become so used to walking by night and living in an apartment darkened by blackout curtains that light was anathema. I was half-way to turning already, I thought, with a smile.

When I returned, I went into Tilly's room and knew I was doing the right thing. Here was a being that had existed for hundreds, perhaps even thousands, of years. A being that had the capacity for adult thought and yet wanted to be surrounded by children's toys; a being that wanted permanent nursing and care. It was perverse. I definitely didn't need this creature in my life. Once I had her power, I would be free to finally be myself, to be successful. I wouldn't be cramped by the constant reminders of my own mortality, by the sound of the clock ticking ever closer to death, to failure. I'd have all the time in the world to reinvent myself as a masterpiece.

She remained sound asleep as I prepared the equipment, lightly tapped her forearm, stuck her with the needle and sucked up a syringe full of her condition. Handling it carefully, I went to the bathroom, wrapped the tourniquet around my arm and injected myself with Tilly's blood. Immediately, I felt a surge of energy rush through me. As the seconds passed and the foreign substance began to circulate, it felt better than any drug I'd ever taken. My limbs felt free of the aches that had increasingly weighed down on them of late. My head felt clear, free of either the fog of melancholy or Tilly's psychic grasp. I looked in the mirror and examined my face. I may have just been imagining it but my skin seemed no longer sallow but pure white, like ivory. I felt alive.

I walked into the bedroom. I knew exactly what I wanted to do. I was horny as Hell so I tore off the bedsheets and virtually pounced on Anna.

'Adam?' she said, rubbing her eyes. 'What's going on? What are you doing?'

'Let's fuck,' I hissed. 'Let's fuck like we're teenagers, Moneypenny.'

She rolled her eyes but gave a noise of assent and I forced myself into her. I began thrusting; powerful, deep lunges that felt incredible. I got faster and faster and she began to scream out, becoming wetter and wetter with each penetration. I was so carried away and so wrapped up in my own orgasm, I didn't hear Tilly enter the room until she spoke up.

'Oh daddy,' she said. 'You are a fucking idiot.'

I turned around to look at her. Anna had gone completely still beneath me. I laughed. 'Really? I'm the idiot? Look at me. I've got it. I've got whatever it is you've got and it's amazing! I don't need you any more. Go find yourself a new daddy.'

She smiled. 'It doesn't work like that. You do need me. You can't just steal youth like it's some kind of drug. It's given when it's earned.'

'Well, it's working isn't it? I feel fantastic.'

'You're changing, daddy, but not into what you think you are.'

'Yeah, well, I'm sure Anna'll appreciate the…' I stopped cold as I turned back to look down at Anna and saw what I'd done. She was dead. Her crotch was torn to pieces. I'd been thrusting into what now resembled a pile of shredded chuck steak thrown carelessly into an empty space between her torso and her legs. Litres of blood were already soaking through the sheets and the mattress. I'd murdered her.

'You don't know your own strength, daddy,' said Tilly, with a sense of menace.

I leapt off the bed and grabbed my head in despair. I didn't hear or feel it rip, but when I took my hands away, they were filled with my own hair. I touched the hair on my chest and that too was loose. It was dropping from my body and onto the floor. I screamed as I realised my teeth were wobbling. I put my hand up to my mouth to stop them but it was no use. I felt them roll around my mouth like mints and had to spit them out before I swallowed them.

My gums ached as two sharp new teeth burst through at the front. I scrambled past Tilly and back into the bathroom to look at myself in the mirror. I was a monster. My skin was bright white and completely smooth but my features were distorted and unrecognisable. I had just the two sharp teeth at the front of my mouth, protruding obscenely from between my grey lips. My eyes were solid black. I curled up into a ball on the floor and screamed until I had no feeling in my throat.

Now we live in the darkness together. Tilly keeps me around like a pet and treats me as an amusement at best. It will be a while before she fully forgives me for what I did. She is far stronger than me mentally but she needs my physical might. She keeps me on a psychic leash. I kill for her but I'm not allowed to drink the blood. She feeds me offal when I get too sick. I live on kidneys, livers, lungs. Sometimes I just want to walk out into the sunlight and embrace the fire but I have too much responsibility. I accept that it's my own fault that I am what I am; a grotesque, dreadful failure. All that's left for me is to make sure Tilly is healthy, that she continues to live. Her life is my life. I never wanted it this way but at least, amongst the blood and the chaos and the humiliation of my great mistake, I have purpose. It's not much but it's mine.